The Gardener

Eliza Galvez

Published by New Generation Publishing in 2021

First Edition

ISBN: 978-1-80031-703-1

www.newgeneration-publishing.com

New Generation Publishing

Preface

The Gardener is semi-autobiographical, written with emotions that are purely my own but transferred to my hero. Fact and fiction are intimately woven throughout, but not all real incidents are related as they happened.

I adapted this piece of history through my mother's story and fiction-alised it so that I could include my love of the cultures and traditions I experienced in my childhood, which I hope will be a legacy, a reference and a throwback to the days when twenty centavo given as pocket money from my grandmother was a treat… the nostalgic past.

The story was stored for years, my scribbled thoughts in pieces of paper tucked randomly between book pages and diaries, drawers and plastic envelopes, waiting to burst into life as a book. It was my affinity for all things Japanese that took me to the Japanese tea ceremony in Cambridge, where the sky magically opened the road to my writing journey. My experience has been full of positive superlatives, but meeting and staying with the granddaughter of my hero and her family in Miyazaki, Japan, was where I found my real Pearl of the Orient.

Behind the new life I found in my writing, my hero was a Japanese military officer who was sent to Mindanao in the Philippines before the war, whose father and grandfather's fate is still unknown. It is my goal that, within my 'book life', it will create public awareness to help me find a missing soldier.

"Remember the lotus flower… Even though it plunges to life from beneath the mud, it does not allow the dirt that surrounds it to affect its growth or beauty."
(From: *Rise Up and Salute the Sun* by Suzy Kassem)

The lotus flower is symbolic of re-birth and self-regeneration, with its fascinating will to live being a religious symbol of enlightenment and purity.

The story of *The Gardener*, just like the lotus flower, reflects his rise above the human destruction caused by the war. It illustrates, despite the murky impurities around him, how the beauty of loyalty and true friendship can triumph over the heartlessness of war.

A Trunk is Just a Box

Shigehiro's Trunk

Marta looked at the object in front of her and whispered to herself, "A trunk is just a box but a trunk with a lock is a box with a secret".

On the floor was a large brown wooden trunk. To her, it seemed like a sealed cage that protected the fragile contents inside it. It was enclosed, with metal strips hammered securely in place at intervals along its solid body, and securely locked with an equally strong padlock that no human hands would dare try to open without its key.

She knelt in front of the wooden trunk, with a key in her hand. She had longed for the day when she could unbolt the heavy metal bar across it to reveal what was hidden inside the mysterious box. She stared, motionless with curiosity, her head spinning with excitement; she was wide eyed, fixated on the object. Her fingers trembled with anticipation. The Gardener's most cherished possession was at her fingertips, which would allow her to lift the veil that protected the person behind the disguise.

As the morning sun streamed through the holes on the dilapidated remains of the tea house, she felt hot yet refreshed by the sweetness of the morning air. The noisy early morning vendors, and even the smell of decaying leaves that lay thickly on the ground, brought immeasurable comfort to her. Her children skipped enthusiastically on their way to school despite the sad memories of their last night with Shigehiro. Even the slow running stream, *Sapa,* along the side of the church suggested calm, just like the composed natives undeterred by being faced with the mass effort of clearing the ruins left by the war.

The tea house stood intact to represent the embodiment of the person that he was, his legacy; it was the only place where he lived true to himself. His beloved garden, with flowering plants, and its symbolic stone path and rocks; his abundant harvest of vegetables; the tactile moss and scented herbs; the wash-basin and the lanterns: everything was a pleasant reminder of a person whose presence brought delight and harmony to a very traditional village.

Marta sobbed with despair, for she could never imagine that there would ever be another person like Shigehiro. She got up and looked around the tea house for any reminder, any piece of something she could hold and put close to her aching heart and help her ignore the truth of his absence - his departure.

Then, she remembered his kimono. She jumped up with hurried steps to the closet and, as if the angels saw her weeping heart, she was granted with his perfectly restored silk kimono. She felt her woeful tears on her cheeks soon erased by the quiet elation of a laughter from inside her. Then an involuntary scream burst as if her lungs had needed the release ever since the moment she stepped into the tea house.

"Yes, yes, yes, his kimono! You're mine now, forever! Oh, how a brief moment of joy can replace a long morning of sadness."

Instantly, her thoughts transported her back to that magical day when they first met.

That indelible day was picture-framed in her memory: the day he unbolted their gate, the day he arrived at their house, the day he opened the gate to his new life in *Barrio Obrero*. She suddenly felt a shiver, a haunting black cloud formed as her thoughts brought her back to the unforeseen events of the unforgettable black years of their lives. To her, it was like a bad dream, a nightmare. Still crystal-clear as she tried to erase the dreadful episode of her past from her mind; how the cruelty of the war changed everything. If only her melancholy desires could bring back the years she had with the gardener, Shigehiro Yoshida.

For her, it was impossible to forget the echoes of his presence as they lingered with warm feelings that were still contained within her heart. The night he left for the war and became a Japanese soldier for the Imperial Army, she thought, was the night she closed that chapter of her life with him.

His return, the trunk and the tea house were all too painful reminders, but they were also true testaments of his existence in her life. She desperately tried to separate them from her life but found it hard to resist the deep impressions that he left. Like the pages of a book, her story remained unopened but intact and sealed. Shaking with hesitant anxiousness, and terrified of what was inside the trunk, she momentarily paused and knelt down to say a prayer. It was not enough for her to ask for divine courage, but she was scared and would never allow her family to be hurt in any way. Opening the box to reveal its contents would uncover the fragile secrets of a soldier.

"I remember," she whispered to herself. "I remember that day!"

It was a fairly quiet day, a dull early September afternoon. The intense heat and high humidity of the summer had gradually turned to cool mornings and evenings. It was a time of calm, in both the city and the village households, before the frantic activities that preceded Christmas.

Marta was in her garden, taking a

leisurely afternoon walk before the children arrived from school and in preparation of the usual commotion before the family dinner. It was her quiet moment, this much awaited daily stroll around her garden to be in the company of her heavenly plants. She was suddenly disturbed when she heard the gate handle creak as it moved. Curious, her steps led her towards the gate, then she cautiously stopped in front of it to see who it was on the other side.

Slightly opened, she noticed the chubby masculine hand tightly gripping the iron gate to lessen the noise. Silence followed the stranger's light footsteps as he stepped inside, unnoticed. Then, a tired-looking but smartly dressed man in a dark brown linen suit appeared from the other side of the gate and stood in front of her, clutching a small straw bag.

Surprised by the unexpected visitor at her doorstep so late in the afternoon, she became irritated by the incon-venience imposed on her crucial schedule of garden inspection.

"A Chinese vendor! Except this man has nothing to sell, not a single basket of anything, so what does he want?"

She seemed annoyed with an edgy agitation in her voice as she quietly asked herself, hoping for his instan-taneous exit.

Barrio Obrero

Barrio Obrero

The stranger stood straight like a bamboo pole, then bent slowly from his waist down to almost forty-five degrees and carried on in slow action until his face almost touched his knees. Then, in reverse movement, he gently curled up into an upright position and completed his greeting. Marta could almost feel every vertebra in his spine being stretched. She nearly fell over herself just looking at him as he adjusted his short, sturdy but beautifully balanced body. His first words broke the silence: "She like a job for me?"

He bowed again. She scrutinised the diminutive figure in front of her, her eyes fixed on the stranger, completely hypnotised by his presence.

Marta asked him to step inside then pointed at the front door. He followed with his head firmly focused on the ground, moving his head from side to side, and glanced at the garden as he passed by. He glided across the marble floor, with silent steps easing him to his seat.

Marta could not contain her curiosity, so she thoughtfully continued her assessment of the stranger. As she looked at him with approval, she decided that, without a doubt, this man cared for his image. This man presented himself with an utmost diligence about his persona, from head to toe, starting at the top with his cleanly shaven face, with not a hair out of place, and the short toothpaste-white fingernails. Despite the intense heat, there was not a bead of sweat in sight.

Her eyes were still drawn to his face. She noticed he had big elephantine ears and, just below the left lobe, there was a reddish patch that looked like a birthmark. His tiny nostrils went hand and hand with his miniature nose. His bushy eyebrows highlighted his tiny eyes. His pale complexion looked as delicate as his thin rosebud lips, lightly dusted with a tinge of dusky pink.

Daydreaming of the charismatic figure in front of her, Marta's thoughts were interrupted when he spoke with gentle persuasion.

"My name is Shigehiro. Please allow me to be your servant."

Without hesitation, she brought him to their household and into their lives.

* * *

He had his first restful night's sleep in *Barrio Obrero* right until he was woken up by the bright sunlight that streamed through the opaque *capiz* shell window. The heat had already permeated through the wooden walls and, coupled with the buzz and noise around him, the unfamiliar surroundings made him eager to get up and explore his new home.

"So, this is *Barrio Obrero?*" he whispered to himself, observing the commotion outside at four o'clock in the morning. Lively as a cattle market, he thought that it was definitely a very different picture and sound of early morning life to the time he had spent in Cebu.

Barrio Obrero was a small suburb of Manila, about thirty minutes *calesa* (a horse drawn carriage) ride to the heart and centre of the country's capital. Sparsely populated, it still had a thriving community with a tightly knit neighbourhood, whose lives centred on the church.

The day started for most natives as early as four in the morning when local street vendors navigated their way from house to house, selling everything from food to beds. Heads, carrying heavy-laden baskets, hurtled around the empty streets. A dawn chorus of vending men and women shouted as they paraded the narrow alleys passing each other, hoping

10

a housewife would be in need of their tempting selection of food on offer.

Filipinos, well known for their love affair with food, had their culture embedded in their minds and ingrained in their hearts and souls. This was highlighted by their countless religious celebrations and *fiestas,* which were essentially central to their daily lives.

Freshly baked bread, called *pan de sal* (sweet white buns), was sold first thing in the morning, whereas fish, shellfish, seafood, vegetables, fruits and meat were all available from mid-morning. Other perishables, such as homemade cheese, *kesong puti* (white cheese) and *taho* (sweet soya bean curd drink) followed the morning line up when *merienda* (a mid-morning snack) continued the daily parade around eleven in the morning. This is when the sun's intense heat released its most uncomfortable temperature and the body slowed down to drag the natives to the comfort of their afternoon nap or *siesta.*

Meals were cooked three times a day for the family, so a steady supply of ingredients were on hand and, even for late evening snacks, there were no shortages of choices. A favourite delicacy made from duck's embryo and called *balut* was sold warm till midnight. There was also *sitcharon* (fried pig's skin), warm boiled peanuts, sweet toffee bananas and native *suman* – these were glutinous rice or cassava wrapped in banana leaves and served with freshly grated coconut, all too tempting for the

11

palate that disregarded any dietary discipline.

As well as food, throughout the day, it was a common scene to see household and furniture vendors loitering in the narrow streets. Blankets, sleeping mats (*banig*), mosquito nets, saucepans, baskets, chairs, baby cots, clothing, carved ornaments and *capiz* (made from shell) lamps were all transported from street to street on wooden carts.

Occasionally, in turtle-pace fashion, bamboo beds were strapped on the vendor's back, carried painstakingly in the midday sun. It was an all-day walking market with the luxury of having all goods brought to your doorstep. Marta had a fish *suki* (favourite vendor), her vegetable *suki,* a cheese *suki* and a bedding *suki.*

* * *

The whole neighbourhood was never still or silent. Even when there was a lull in activity on the streets, somewhere in somebody's back garden cock fights went on with shrieking gamblers that occasionally interrupted afternoon naps or *siestas.* Youngsters made the alleyways their common meeting points or playgrounds. They played in harmony and lived as one big family. Their presence created vibrancy and excitement, which brought substance to the vast arable fields that surrounded the village.

The Garcia family lived in a five-bedroom house, with separate living accommodation for their cook, nurse-maid *(yaya)*, driver and Shigehiro, a welcomed addition to the household, their gardener.

Marta, the family matriarch, was a direct descendant of a Spanish father, a wealthy landowner called Julian Marquez Del Toro, and of a Filipina mother, Felicia Bautista. She was pale skinned, with a porcelain face as fresh as the dusting of morning dew on a newly blossomed *gardenia*. A natural *mestiza*, who dressed herself every day in *baro at saya,* she walked tall with her enviable pencil-thin figure, despite her child-bearing years. Her long, straight black hair was never out of place, tightly brushed back and coiled demurely to a small tidy bun that sat just above the nape of her elegant Spanish neck.

Jaime Garcia, the family patriarch, was a handsome native from the northern part of the Philippines called Bigaa, Bulacan. He was of humble background but well educated. He moved to Manila to work for an insurance broker, one of the many companies in Manila owned by Don Pedro Marquez Del Toro, Marta's brother. It was at Don Pedro's birthday party that they met – a traditional yearly office party shared by his family, friends and employees at his factory grounds and his home at Grace Park in Manila.

Married life suited Marta, who stayed at home with her children: sixteen-year-old Ester, fourteen-year-old Francisco, twelve-year-old Manuel, nine-year-old Rosalina and seven-year-old Benjamin. They lived in the neighbourhood close to her brother, Don Pedro Marquez Del Toro, who owned a shoe factory called *Ang Matibay*.

The Garcia's house was architecturally of Spanish type and built in 1751. It suggested the wealth and status of the era. A two-storey wooden structure, it had a tiled roof, with wood-framed sliding windows inlaid with *capiz* shell and a large wrought-iron balcony that jotted out from the entire width of the front master bedroom and faced the village square. It stood out from the rest of the houses as typical Filipino houses were made of bamboo material and palm leaves called *Bahay Kubo.*

Inside the hard wooden exterior, the family home was enveloped by maternal tenderness and paternal safekeeping through the bible, religious teachings and a devotion to the family church. Family prayer was a disciplined daily routine after family dinner, where the family gathered in the living room, sang hymns and prayed before bed. It was a new religious doctrine, one which Shigehiro had to adopt, reluctantly at first, but eventually blending the ritual with his own.

It was hard for Shigehiro to join in singing so Ester made sure he was not excluded by his language disability. To encourage him, she sat next to him and became his personal singing coach and lyric tutor every night while Rosalina just sat on the other side and held his hand. The two boys were always amused by his strange diction and painful sounding musicality, leaving them giggling deliriously throughout this nightly entertainment.

Sunday, without fail, was focused on church worship. The church bells rang at eight in the morning, like a cock crowing to wake up its congregation. The formal service was at nine and, at eight-thirty sharp, hymns were played at highly amplified volume through the church speakers, specially placed at the church tower to face the village square. This ensured that no one overslept and no one arrived a minute late.

At the Garcia's, the boys fed the horses with Jaime before breakfast. Dressed, exuding excitement and smiles, they brought a ray of cheerfulness to a meadow pasture, bypassing the overgrown weeds and shrubs with baskets full of corn feed. Shigehiro trailed along with them for the first time with a bucket of water.

Sunday was also a time for family lunch gatherings. Relatives near and far came together to emphasise the importance of seeing and being in each other's lives.

Families consisted of mainly five to ten children, so a welcomed tradition of bringing a dish or two was a common practice. As intimate as they were with each family, at certain Sundays the family had lunch with their household helpers.

It was Shigehiro's first Sunday lunch at the Garcia's. Being an outsider, and considering his own opinion about his inadequate skills of natural rapport with humanity, he felt small waves of nerves in his belly. Doreng, the *yaya,* reassured him on his first day that by

15

merely bringing him into their household, the other helpers knew that Marta would have chosen someone that would easily blend in with them. He expressed his knowledge of many practical skills to Marta but, in the end, she thought that it would be good to have a gardener. He was given a job to re-design or transform her dreary old garden and give it a new lease of life.

The Garden

The garden was immediately on the right-hand side of the wrought-iron gate entrance of the house. Once inside, there was a paved area that stretched from the gate to the whole length of the house. This served the purpose of an unmarked boundary between the garden, on the right, and the front door of the house, which was on the left. No visible fence separated the two areas but, in the middle of the patio, there stood a ten-foot-long table which seemed like an endless wooden apparatus for family banquets. It was where Marta and Jaime sat most evenings to read the Bible. A calming combination of the cool breeze and the hypnotic scent from the *Sampaguita* (Philippine jasmine) plant were a nightly dosage of their bedtime sleep-inducing routine.

Marta loved her garden, a dense area of shrubs and trees, with much-loved flowers like arum lilies, scented ginger lily and white plumbago. She was not known for her gardening knowledge but for the sheer love of the plants she continuously bought; she chose and was guided only by her instinct during her regular visits at the nearest market. She collected them for their shape, colour or scent, but mainly to provide a place for plants that she loved. The garden was not shaped nor divided into borders, not even planted with a particular purpose, but it was in her nature simply to collect and nurture plants and that was a good enough reason for her.

Some of the plants died from over-watering or from a lack of water, others died from her inadequate knowledge of how to position her specimens in the garden – but some died for no reason at all. It was an inexplicable mystery that puzzled her to absolute desperation. And yet, she considered it her pride and joy to take every visitor to the house on an exclusive garden tour before entering the front door.

Her passion was not always viewed with approval, as others saw her garden as an area simply represented with layers of green leaves and brown stems. Despite the hidden pleasures of its tactility and scents, as highlighted by the *Sampaguita* and *ilang ilang* trees, visitors rarely took time to appreciate them.

The *Sampaguita* gave her joy as it thrived in all conditions and rewarded her with clusters of white buds that burst into highly scented multi-petalled flowers that came as regularly as the rainy season. Belonging to the jasmine family, it is a low-growing shrub with thick stems and dark curly leaves. Famously used in perfume and teas, it was the national flower of the Philippines. The flowers can be threaded into a scented necklace, which over the years had been used as a flower garland. This traditional freshly threaded flower adorned men and women's necks during special occasions and celebrations but delightfully it was accepted as a fragrant welcome kiss for the guest that entered the host's home.

On the north east of the property, Marta had a mini orchard of tropical fruit trees. Locally they are called, *mangga, macopa, suha, duhat* and *kasoy.* Sheltering the trees from extreme weather were a line of the sturdy trunks of coconut trees that stood along the back and the sides of the plot. Coconut trees come in three varieties but a particular favourite was the *macapuno,* the sweetest variety of the coconut family, with transparent jelly-like flesh that is used for making desserts.

A regular unwritten timetable in her routine, every afternoon before dusk saw her relax in the garden before the children came back from school. School finished at four when *yaya* Doreng walked them back home and much-welcomed help from Shigehiro became the highlight of their end of day walk home. The two young boys took turns to sit on his shoulder all the way back, a much-needed relief for tired little legs.

Marta liked to walk to each plant, eyes down, closely examining them for signs of a tiniest growth or flower that might encourage her that she was green fingered. So, when the new gardener told her that the garden would have a total makeover, she was delighted. The morning of the day Shigehiro started to work towards the new garden, he woke up earlier than usual and well before sunrise. He had a big gleaming smile that sparkled on his face like a burst of morning sunshine. He had grown up surrounded by tropical plants dotted everywhere in his village in Miyazaki.

The row of multi-coloured bougainvillea arched like a rainbow along the path that coloured the narrow streets on his way home. The delicately scented white stamens of the *camia* (wild ginger) flower lit his way on dark evenings. His memories of home felt so distant, yet he was transported back there as he pulled out the sketches of his garden plan.

The plan had started to germinate the day he saw the yard. It was a piece of land beyond the existing garden. A wilderness filled with wild sweet potatoes, cassava and yam, with a solitary Tamarind tree that stood at the end marking the end of the plot at the Garcia Lopez's property.

He knew he needed to beg for help from every able man in the village. The ground had to be dug, heavy stones and rocks needed to be lifted and positioned, bamboo poles needed to be cut, wooden frames had to be made and tied together to make up the fence panels; there were countless little jobs required to put together and bring into reality the plan he had formed on paper. After all, a new project and a purposeful daily focus brought excitement to the mundane tasks of general garden maintenance and upkeep.

Shigehiro's vision was to create a Japanese-style garden. He vowed to make it appealing to everyone in the family but, for Marta, he would provide her with an orderly way of presenting her favourite plants as the focal point of appreciation. Marta's desire for her garden to be revived from deterioration and total demise gave her hope so she willingly accepted his ideas. A hut-like structure was to be added at the top end to create a place for relaxation, tranquillity and a viewing platform for the garden. There would also be a separate place for him to indulge in his culture's way of drinking tea – a Japanese tea house.

The cool early October morning brought eager workmen at sunrise to the doorstep of the Garcia's front gate. Mindful of the possible hot temperature by lunchtime, they arrived with pickaxes, shovels and saws and gathered by the old low bamboo garden fence. It was hardly visible as shrubs had pushed their leafy stems and thick branches through the gaps, which allowed complete dominance along the fence. Work started by pulling and digging out unwanted plants and debris throughout. It was a backbreaking job as the dry unused land was a solid mass of earth, which became a dumping ground for all unwanted solid matter. By the end of the morning, all of the nine-man brigade of garden volunteers had cleared the plot and got it ready to be marked into sections and shaped into well-defined areas.

By noon there was a welcome breath of relief for the men when they all sat down. Lunch had been personally supervised by Marta to make sure that the men were well-fed and energised for the afternoon session of hard manual work. For lunch she served kare *kare*, her signature dish, where she combined ox meat with vegetables such as *pusong saging*, *petchay*, *talong* and *sitaw* in a thick reddish-orange tomato-based sauce of crushed peanuts and shrimp paste, served with boiled rice. Plates were licked clean but the men made room for an energy boosting dessert called *leche flan,* a much sweeter version of creme caramel.

Before lunch was over, truckloads of gravel, rocks and stones in various shapes and sizes were delivered, together with plants Shigehiro had carefully selected for the garden.

A Japanese garden is an interpretation of a borrowed landscape. Visual harmony runs throughout, which includes symmetry, enclosure, balance and symbolism. Rocks, gravel and water are all unifying elements of a Japanese garden, and because the presence of still water is a favourite habitat for mosquitoes, he decided to have a stone urn with fresh rain water instead of a pond. He looked around to give a final approval of his plan and felt proud that the empty space would be replaced by plants chosen specifically for their texture, colour, shape and height to create a scene as a whole that was visually logical and calming.

Having digested the heavy meal and had an hour's rest, with a quick nap for a couple of the men, the afternoon started by pulling down the old knee-high fence. The plants that surrounded the perimeter were dug and put aside for replanting. The empty land was marked into a series of sections, each outlined by strings that corresponded the desired shape. The outlined sections required some contouring of the very flat ground so rocks were deliberately chosen and placed to complement the plants. Outside these sections, and to link all the elements together, a series of irregularly shaped stones were placed to provide a stepping stone path to the tea house.

This was a teamwork job with two or three men working to strategically place each stone, each of which represented nature and evoked senses and emotion. It was important that Shigehiro shared his thoughts and ideas with the men he worked with. These daily exchanges of cultural wisdom became a common ground of conversation and promoted an affinity towards each other's culture.

Finally, barrows full of earth were spread to fill the gaps in between the big rocks and along the path. Altogether, he thought that it was a physically demanding day for all of them but, emotionally satisfied to see the beginning of a marriage of two cultures coming together, he was glad to see them all working as one big happy family.

Day two began with all the men sat on the marble floored patio, cutting strips of the pre-measured bamboo sticks and poles needed for the entrance gate to the new garden. They sat cross-legged and barefooted on the cool patio slabs with fingers and toes working at regular intervals to weave a lattice pattern to form rectangular panels. The wooden strips and poles were held firmly together by *abaca* hemp.

This was a craft built on from early

manhood as the basis of the basic carpentry required to build homes at that time. They used thick bamboo trunks as poles, which kept them erect. The poles were held with the native hemp called *abaca*. *Abaca* are fibres extracted from the *abaca* plant: a plant related to the banana family. The entire construction of the fence was left to the locals while Shigehiro just looked on to admire their nimble fingers working with artistry and dexterity. He was consumed by their skills and the insight he was gaining into their local lives and heritage, and he confessed to the men how he looked forward for dawn every day for his apprenticeship training in the culture of the Philippines.

Their day was devoted to everything related to the role of the noble bamboo plant and all its parts. Once the fences were put up, they worked on the seating area, an arbour to hold the climbing plants, a thatched entrance gate and, finally, a combined effort from all the men to build the tea house. When they were at the last stages of finishing their day, and still in a light-hearted spirit, Shigehiro was totally bemused by an outburst of enchanting medleys of Philippine songs that erupted from the lungs of music-loving Filipinos.

***

The following day, men congregated as before on the patio, waiting for Shigehiro to come out with his plan of the day. He was normally up and at the gate before the first man arrived.

Bright and eager, with a welcoming bow, the men had adapted the Japanese courtesy as their reply. It was nearly seven when Doreng, the housemaid, came out to announce that Shigehiro was in bed, and very ill. She explained further that, "He had been suffering from acute abdominal pain and discomfort from vomiting. He spent the night tossing and turning in his bed and, from the early hours of the morning, he had diarrhoea and green vomit."

Shocked and speechless, the men stepped outside the house gate with disappointment and sadness, but they resigned themselves to staying close in case help was needed.

Inside the house, Shigehiro was instantly confined to a bedroom alone with only Doreng to attend to all his needs. Strict sanitation was the priority and everyone, especially the children who were lost without him, was totally banned from being anywhere near his room.

He was dizzy due to extreme loss of fluid, which had also caused his low blood pressure. He felt faint and disoriented from lack of food and water from his body. Doreng was quick to recognise the symptoms and immediately suspected that he might have Cholera.

As the answer to extreme dehydration, she knew that fluid replacement with salt was the best cure as a home remedy. She sat with him, following careful hygiene procedures, and nursed him in and out of sleep for three days. She felt her hands become paper dry from endless soap and water scrubs that were a necessary discipline to protect herself from being infected. The room felt like an oven from the boiled water being brought into the room, despite all the windows being wide open, which allowed fresh air and ventilation. There were moments when she felt choked, uncomfortably thinking about the germs that floated around her, ready to infect her body in an instant as punishment for any brief lapse from her strict hygiene regime.

The Garcia family mourned for the loss of activity and sparkle. Marta spent mornings and evenings on her knees, praying, and she sang hymns and read the Bible to comfort him. Ester was equally distressed and, as for the boys, they cried at every mealtime. How they felt missing him at the table was beyond their understanding. For them, a cough and a cold were how they measured illness, but to be confined in bed, unseen for more than two days, was so depressing that they wanted it to go away very soon.

Undeterred by the unfortunate circumstances, the local men turned up every morning with a hearty optimism that they would find Shigehiro up, ready and waiting for them. Yet day after day of disappointment did not stop them and, instead of the men being armed with garden tools, they brought him fruit, vegetables, chicken and eggs for the nutritional healing of his poorly body.

They waited each day until Doreng gave them a detailed picture of his condition and each morning they left with hope that his small figure would appear in the village square the following day.

Jaime Garcia was particularly worried about the ill state that had befallen him, especially in the absence of any close family around him. He was concerned that no one was there to comfort him in this difficult time. So, that night, he asked Doreng for her opinion on Shigehiro's state of health before he went to bed.

Feeling optimistic he would see some small sign of recovery, early the next day, Jaime decided to see him before going to work. He got up in plenty of time and asked Doreng to make up a soup of rice with shredded ginger. Then he took it, piping hot, to Shigehiro's room and spoon fed him until the bowl was empty.

Work seemed unimportant to him; keeping someone alive was more useful than being in a room full of businessmen chasing their commissions. That afternoon, he wanted to fly home to his friend's company and, although life seemed to have temporarily left him, the family longed for his recovery. Together every night with Marta, they both knelt in prayer for their helpless friend.

Everyone stuck to their routine of strict sanitation, regular fluid intake and the gradual introduction of small easily digestible ingredients to his rice soup, and they saw daily positive changes. It took nearly six days before he could stand up and walk around his bedroom, suggesting he had regained some of his strength, offering reassurance of his recovery.

By this time, Doreng got to know him literally inside and out. She sponged him clean, undressed and changed his sweaty pyjamas, brushed his teeth and powdered his weak body with Johnson's talcum powder to keep him fresh and cool. They almost lived together, as there were times when it was necessary for her to stay with him all night, especially during the critical stages of his sickness. When, finally, he uttered his first words at the end of his series of vomiting, he looked at his faithful nurse and said to her, "I will build a statue of you in the garden as a symbol of my gratitude to you and to all… to whom I owe my life."

Alone in bed that night, he tossed and turned, for the first time in a week, but this time with a stomach cramp that felt like a stabbing pain. *Death would be sweeter than to reveal who I really am*; his thought of dishonoured loyalty brought along a fear that he wanted to vomit all the ugly green slime of disgust from inside his belly. He stared at the ceiling, with a plan to wake up before anyone and take the *jungle bolo*, the native garden scythe from the garden shed, and end his life with dignity. It would be an honourable act by a disgraced traitor who was about to betray sincere friendship.

Morning brought blinding light to his sensitive eyes. He had not seen sunlight in so many days and he felt woozy and unsteady as he walked towards the garden. Thoughts of his days at sea before being rescued in Cebu came flooding back with the same sensation of uncertainty and confusion. Doubtful of what he was about to carry out, he headed out to where he could see the entrance gate of the fresh layout of the garden, and to the other end where the tools were kept. Guided only by a headful of guilt, tears rolled down his pale and sunken face as he grabbed the long razor-sharp tool, shaped like a form of bayonet, from the wall. He held it tightly between his closed palms in a samurai fashion. Shigehiro placed the edge of the blade against his stomach, slightly piercing his skin then knelt on the bare ground, with courage and the resolve that his action was more noble than shameful.

The sound of the first cock crowing signalled a new day. It felt like a wakeup call that brought him back to the light from a very dark place. The strong suicidal thoughts left him and emptied the guilt that had nested in his head for over twelve hours.

The cloudless sky and the space around him were all whiter than he had ever seen before. "So, there is a God who looks down and decides what is best for us. There must be a good reason to forbid anyone from performing such a noble act," he whispered reluctantly to himself.

For whatever reason, and not knowing why, Shigehiro found himself walking back to his room. A firmness returned to his step, with a renewed energy as he got dressed then went out to see if any of the village's men were around. He was

determined to reassure them that he was
back from his battle with death.

The Garden and Tea House

The Garden

Barrio Obrero was also awake. Most of the daily vendors had finished their early morning rounds and the next shift had begun with baskets full of *merienda,* a selection of mid-morning snacks from a variety of sticky rice cakes, usually cooked in coconut milk to *sitcharon* (pork scratching), to peanuts or a soya drink called *taho* and *suman*. *Suman* is a glutinous rice cake wrapped in banana leaves which comes in many forms, colours and flavours, a favourite choice for the mid-morning snack.

Usually each town had its own speciality, each competing for taste, colour and texture. Served with sugar from sugar cane and topped with grated young coconut flesh.

Shigehiro was not alone in the square for any longer than a heartbeat when *Kaka Kiko* arrived. *Kaka* is a term of respect for someone elderly. They exchanged bows, which the locals had welcomed as a means of respect when greeting their Japanese friend. The reunion of the two men promptly became an assembly of men. They followed him to the Garcia house and began to develop their plan of constructing the tea house.

The tea house would be a structure similar to the Filipino *bahay-kubo,* but with a complete transition of its interior to mimic a Japanese tea room. The location was pre-planned and had to be at the end of the garden, enclosed by the dense planting of bamboo for privacy and isolation.

The group of men looked down at the drawing on the ground in front of them and, with a unanimous nod of approval, they agreed that it could be built in three days. Shigehiro's face lit up with an ear-to-ear smile, but it quickly disappeared when he realised that the number of *tatami* mats dictated the size of the structure.

He realised that it would have to be a task in reverse. Before they could plan how big the house would be, they would have to find the *tatami* mats first. Then Shigehiro burst out loud in a scream and said, "*Mitate,* yes. That's how it has to be!"

The men were confused, totally discombobulated.

"Authentic tatami mats can be substituted for the local equivalent," he explained. Given the circumstances, with the absence of the true material, the local *banig* would be given a new role. Delighted, locals gathered layers upon layers of palm leaves and, together with their wives, they sat in their homes to weave a square each for the tea house. It was a local project and they rose to the challenge with justifiable pride. The new *tatanig (*Philippine *banig* adapted as Japanese *tatami)* was created.

Shielded by the thick, leaning branches of bamboo trees, the men stood as they admired what they had built: a solitary modified *bahay kubo*, alternatively known as the tea house. A tea house is the cultural home of the Japanese tea ceremony. It is an activity involving the preparation and presentation of *matcha* – powdered green tea. It is a ritual to cleanse the mind and induce inner peace, confined in a small space facilitated by quiet meditation without any distractions.

Shigehiro discussed and negotiated with Marta at lengths during many afternoons of planning the garden. In the end, Marta had to succumb to his explanations and agreed. A series of rustic stepping stones were laid that led to the hut. The path leading to the tea house was lined by five lanterns. Generally, tea ceremonies took place in the evening and lanterns would help him find his way to the tea house.

The construction of the Japanese garden started by marking and reshaping the ground into each of the five sections. The entrance to the garden was through a gate, followed by a series of winding stepping stones in irregular sizes and shapes, chosen particularly to feature texture with well-defined shapes to marry with the plants within each section.

To the right of the gate, immediately at knee height, was a section that had three low aromatic herbs, oregano for scent and touch, along with two local grasses, called *makahiya* (mimosa pudica). It was designed to give the two young boys interesting specimens. Following the path, an arbour was constructed with a bamboo seat where, on both sides and above, he planted climbing plants – the highly scented *Dama de Noche* and femininely pink flowering strands of *Cadena de Amor* (antigonon leptopus) intertwined with the distinctive smell of the flowering Philippine garlic vine, with its large purple bell-shaped blooms that smelled of garlic. It was Marta's favourite viewing spot, a shady rest stop where she absorbed the pleasures of the delightfully metamorphosed garden.

At the top end, just before the tea house, were placed a group of grasses, ferns (*Dapo,* Bird's Nest fern) and broad leaf plants, which included the local taro variety called *gabi* and the native purple flowering ground orchid. On approaching the tea house, to soften the boundary, were a row of *rosal* (gardenias) just before the hut, on the other side of the fence. Then, immediately on the right-hand side, was a water basin, a *tsukubai,* where rain water was collected and used for cleansing the face and mouth before entering the tea house.

Entering the garden from the left of the entrance gate, low-growing white, light pink and a bright pink *kalachuchi* (frangipani) were grouped together for colour accent. Behind the low growing Plumeria, or Frangipani plants, a white mussaenda philippica stood at the back, which then led to a group of carefully chosen big rocks, placed as architectural symbols. These were surrounded by low growing dense moss that looked like massive green pin cushions. Three *camia* (ginger lily) plants, with arching strap-like leaves contrasted by its delicate silk butterfly-shaped petals, highlighted by its alluring scent, were the crowning glory of this section of the garden. The gardener sat in front of this, his favourite plant, for hours to absorb its beauty, which reminded him of his home in Miyazaki. Then, behind the rocks, the magnificent and fragrant ilang ilang tree, with its strong woody branches, towered serenely above the rest of the garden to perfume the air below it.

Mossy grass (zoysia matrella), mixed with the common grass called *carabao* grass (paspalum renggeri), covered the ground and created a calming mass of green carpet, but it was also used as a backcloth for the plant, setting and framing each section for the viewer. Five lanterns were accurately spaced at interval to provide light and guide him to the tea house on dark evenings.

In the design of his Japanese garden, its main elements – rocks, gravel, water features and specially selected plants were all planted within its boundaries. He managed to incorporate the elements found within his home using species of trees native to the Philippines, bamboos, flowers, ferns and grasses, within each enclosure, where paths, stepping stones, lanterns, Buddha, a water basin and an arbour brought together harmony that suggested nature in a borrowed landscape. One could picture a forest, a waterfall and the influence of Zen religion within the space. He created an oasis of calm and peacefulness within what was once neglected and forgotten. The flat and uninteresting field was turned into a mirror image of a garden in Japan

The Japanese garden stood proud, as if a spiritual landscaper magically dropped the finished garden from above. It was an outdoor space with meaning and a sense of purpose. Its aesthetic simplicity meant every plant was placed to serve a unified, harmonious and poetic picture. Each viewing position was framed. The paths were designed to weave around a garden that encouraged Marta to sit, observe and contemplate each section like a painting.

From the viewing platform of the tea house, numerous birds cawed and sang as they flew over the canopy of trees. The stillness was only broken by the rustling of leaves as the wind blew while the animal chorus of sounds completed the enchantment that surrounded him. It was a special and poetic moment as he walked around the garden. Then he picked up a fallen leaf, caressed a blade of grass, fingered every hair on a moss stone and stared, bewitched by the sparkling red tips on each petal of a flower. Every little detail inspired him to write a poem dedicated to his newly-embraced garden and home, *Barrio Obrero*.

Delicate Camia
Open my eyes, see the world.
Fragrant white *Rosal*
Perfumes my body and soul.

When I close my eyes
Sampaguita lights my way.
Breathe the air and live
Float my body to the clouds.

Tall, slender bamboo
Sways and dances to please me.
Leaves move to the wind
Like music I heard before.

Coconuts and palms
Ubiquitous, staple need.
Palm leaves like fingers
Stems like arms that embrace me.

Ilang Ilang trees
Waling Waling with roots.
Cling to hug me
Happiness forevermore.

The moment of bliss he felt would not be complete without the company of the Garcia family and all the people who gave their time, energy and skills in transforming the garden and building the tea house. That late afternoon in October, it was decided between the gardener, the Garcias and everyone in the village that Sunday lunch would take place in the square. There was a sacrificial roast pig on a spit or *lechon* and it was followed by *macapuno* (sweet and tender young coconut) ice cream for everybody!

Tea Ceremony

The Tea Room

The following week was exceptionally
quiet, especially after last Sunday's
merriment in the village square. It
involved nearly everyone's uninhibited
display of song and dance movements until
the early hours of the morning. Anyone
walking into it would have mistaken it
for the celebration at the wedding at
Cana or the feast to glorify the return
of the prodigal son.

That Monday, Shigehiro asked Marta to
come to the tea-house for the first time.

He wanted to give her the pleasures of the sights and colours of the new garden from the viewing platform. Then he could introduce her to the Japanese way of tea, the Japanese tea ceremony.

A tea ceremony is held in a *sukiya* (tea-house), a straw hut. The special occasion was in celebration of the completion of the new tea house. On this formal occasion, the host always wears a kimono. The kimono is the traditional and formal clothing worn, subdued and conservative to avoid any external distraction in order to facilitate inner peace for the individuals. Marta was intrigued when she was asked to wear her traditional dress.

"I would like to share with you a very sacred Japanese tradition. For this, we wear our formal clothes – a *kimono.* May I ask you to wear your formal clothes too, please?" This was followed by his polite bow, and Marta agreed. She waited for a particular day when the house was quiet, making sure that no one was in the house so she could sneak out in her best *saya.*

Saya, short for *baro* (dress) and *saya* (skirt), is a traditional Filipino dress worn only at rare occasions, such as weddings, christenings and at church. Made from pineapple prolifically grown all over the country, with a particular town outside Manila designated only for growing pineapples, called *Las Pinas*. The process sees the painstakingly picking the thorny and leathery leaves, followed by the equally back-breaking scraping of each individual leaf to extract the fibres into delicate fine threads that are normally woven on a hand loom. The *saya* is an outfit for the women, which is combined with a *camisa* or *baro* (the top) and the *saya* or *tapis* (skirt) with the *panuelo* (scarf), an embroidered accessory to adorn a woman's neck.

Marta felt uneasy but oozing with excitement inside as she stepped out of the side door, through the kitchen, and then crept cautiously across the patio to get to the garden. She selected each steady stone on the path on her way through to the tea house. Entering the tea house required a series of disciplines. Washing to cleanse the mouth and the face using the earthenware basin, a *tsukubai*, using the rainwater that had been collected had to be carried out before stepping inside. Outdoor footwear must be left by the entrance and a Japanese *kimono* was the obligatory costume for this revered moment of tranquillity.

On the outer platform, waiting, was her host. Shigehiro, dressed in his fine, black silk *kimono,* stood regal and handsome as he welcomed Marta with his familiar polite bow greeting.

Marta arrived a little before the appointed time and entered the *yoritsuki*, an interior waiting room where she was asked to store unneeded items such as shoes, umbrella and any personal belongings. She was given a pair of silky soft white socks that pulled just below her knees. He walked ahead of Marta and walked past the preparation

area on the left. She was then led and
guided to another room, the main room of
the *sukiya*.

Shigehiro excused himself while he
arranged all the equipment for making the
tea. Adjacent to the main area was a
small kitchen-like room (*mizuya*), an
anteroom where preparation for making
tea took place. Slatted pieces of bamboo
trunks were nailed together to form a
waist-high shelf that housed his tea
equipment, called *chadogu,* such as
earthenware bowls, a stack of *chakin*
(hemp or linen cloth), *chaire* (tea
caddy), tea scoop and the essential tea
whisk.

The preparation room was separated by
two sliding bamboo panels made with a
series of squares covered with thin
transparent paper. Inside the tea room
was an alcove, a '*tokonoma*' that was
built to hang a scroll. Below it was a
ten-inch hollowed-out bamboo trunk that
contained a sprig of *Sampaguita* flower
and a small trail of spray from the
purple orchid.

The room was screened using two
sliding doors, which separated the main
room from the outer kitchen area. The
soft screening doors were made of a
series of thin pieces of bamboo nailed
together. This formed small squares with
transparent Japanese paper to allow
subtle lighting through the room.

With a cat-like prowl, Marta sniffed
her way in, paused with disbelief as she
entered the main room without any
furniture, which made her wonder why
there was not even a chair for her to

42

sit on. More confusion came after when she realised that she stood on what she knew as *banig*, which covered the entire floor area.

Banig was an essential form of bedding before beds came to the bedrooms. Made from dried palm leaves woven by hand to form a single layer of matted square to cover the floor, big enough for a single person – or a double for two to sleep on. Each family member had one, routinely rolled out at night and rolled up, tidying it out of sight during the day. She was quite content to assume that Shigehiro had a good explanation for such a choice. Shy and puzzled, Marta decided to sit on the floor next to a large trunk. She stroked it to feel relaxed then tried to open the lock. She pushed the button hard but her fragile and delicate little fingers failed to open it.

Bitterly disappointed at not uncovering a possible surprise, she dragged her bottom inch by inch away from the object.

The sound of Shigehiro's shuffling footsteps and the clinking of the tea-making implements on the tray made her abandon her intent. He greeted his guest with a silent bow. This is called *mukae tsuke*. He placed his tray on the floor then proceeded with his precision action of following the procedures of the tea ceremony. The *nigiri-guchi* is the opening into the tea-room – they both almost had to crawl and, as soon as they were inside, they bowed to the *tokonoma,* bowed at the *kakemono* (hanging scroll), bowed again and then she took her place in front of her host and they exchanged greetings.

The host knelt on the floor facing Marta, and he then ritually cleansed each utensil – the tea bowl, whisk and the tea scoop – in a precise order and prescribed motions then placed them in exact arrangement in front of him following the right order of the tea ceremony. When the preparation of the utensils was completed, he then prepared the thick tea.

Koi-cha or thick tea is prepared in a bowl. During this ritual, he meticulously wiped each utensil, rhythmically whisking the green *matcha* powder to its desired consistency, and then the obligatory bows were exchanged between the host and the guest receiving the tea. Marta bowed in return as a gesture of respect to her host, then she was asked to raise the bowl, rotate it, and then to take a sip from the front of the bowl.

After taking sips at slow intervals, and once empty, she was asked to wipe the side of the bowl with a *chakin*, a small rectangular white linen or hemp cloth especially designed to wipe a tea bowl. The bowl was returned to the host, who cleaned it scrupulously, along with all the other equipment, and left the tea room.

Fascinated, Marta had never been part of anything so regimented. She felt exhausted just watching him and, after an hour-long session, she was temporarily paralysed from the waist down because of the long period of kneeling on the floor. Despite the aches and pains in her lower limbs, she got up gently, rubbed her legs and then hobbled towards the stairs.

She felt completely enlightened about the nature of the man that they had brought into their lives. She promised herself to put to bed any mischievous curiosity and walked away relieved at the start of a new stage in their relationship. She left the hut with admiration and rapture at the new way of drinking tea, the Japanese way.

It was almost dark when they exchanged courtesy bows to mark the end of the ritual. Simple, modest, sincere feeling is an integral part of the art. Spiritually and emotionally refreshed, she felt lightheaded as she walked back, full of sparkle and excitement from her experience. She was pleased how Shigehiro was like a shining star that brought new light to the family and the village life. Marta glanced behind her and gave the hut one last look before stepping onto the patio. She sneaked through the kitchen door and ran upstairs to her bedroom for a quick costume change before anyone could see her.

Miyazaki to Cebu

Aoshima-jinja Shrine, Miyazaki

Marta became a regular visitor at the tea house while her children were at school. It became a pattern written in her roster, even her *saya* had found a home in the closet with Shigehiro's kimono. Nearly every day after lunch she quietly left through the back door, then sneaked towards the stepping stones, counting each step to the tea house, followed by a compulsory cleansing of the mouth and face, and walked barefoot once she entered the sliding doors. Green tea was certainly an acquired taste for her, as she coughed and spat out the thick and bitter green liquid a number of times during her first two visits before she finally had the courage to swallow it.

Two weeks with him at the tea house had turned her into a Japanese green-tea-drinking convert. She was fascinated by the Japanese way of drinking tea and was also keen to embrace this exchange of cultures as her return gesture for Shigehiro's efforts in adapting to theirs.

The unseasonal heavy rain started at dawn and, by lunchtime, every inch of the street was covered with water, aided by a night-time darkness that had blanketed the whole village. Strong wind howled and lifted everything off the ground. Deserted streets, with closed windows and empty of human traffic, were a sorry sight for everyone.

Marta, undisturbed by the chaos outside, decided to walk towards the tea house. She walked flat-footedly in the dark, one slow step at a time with a firm grip on each slippery stepping stone. A lantern lit just behind the water urn or *tsukubai* was barely visible but, nevertheless, it gave her just enough light to guide her along. She stooped over the jar of water with two hands and splashed her face and mouth, then her hands.

Shigehiro sat on the floor with his eyes focused on the wooden trunk in front of him. He did not hear the visitor due to the heavy rain hitting the roof, which was quite deafening. She found him as sad as a rabbit in a burrow. he had pieces of cards in one hand and a piece of patterned cloth in the other. Before Marta could speak, he turned over a crumpled piece of card, the only possession he had left, normally keeping it safely his pocket after his unfortunate mishap at sea. He opened his palm to support a fragile photo of his family.

"This is my last photo of my family, just before I left. At this time of the year, it brings an ache in my heart to remember my two sons who died very young.

"In Japan, the fifth of May is what we call *Tango*." He followed on to say, "It is a boys' festival. Girls have the Dolls Festival. The boys have theirs celebrated with cloth carp streamers on poles outside the house and warrior dolls in helmets, placed inside on the stands. Rice cakes and bean jam are wrapped in oak leaf and *'chimaki'* cakes are made of boiled rice and are offered to the dolls.

"It is on this day that people bathe in *shobu-yu* (a bath in which sweet flag leaves are floated) to drive away evil spirits. It is natural that it is used as a flower of the month and during the festival because of its upstanding, sword-like and manly leaves.

"This month, this day, this time, I am reminded of how deeply I miss my family."

He explained further that, in his religion, in Buddhism, the heaven is supposedly to be filled with lotus flowers. It is a common and romantic phrase to say, "Let's meet again in the same lotus flower." It means, "We will meet again in the next life, if you are going to be separated from someone you love." He continued with a distinct voice of optimism then whispered softly as he said these words to Marta.

"Lotus flower in the pond
Lotus flower in the heaven
How wonderful to think in the next life
We will be together again in a lotus
flower."

The sound of the rain outside seemed to have paused as silence filled the room. An empty flow of melancholic air circled around them as Marta froze with sadness. She got up to put her arms around him but he turned away towards the window to hide his tears. He put his head out to see any sign of the storm abating, but it seemed like it was set for the day or even for a week. They both bowed as Shigehiro made his way to the outer room to make tea for both of them.

Marta moved from the floor to a soft cushion while she drank her tea, followed by a piece of sticky rice cake. After collecting all the empty cups and plates, Shigehiro decided that it was time to tell Marta why and how he came to Manila. Usually, their afternoons at the tea house were reserved for drinking tea and, afterwards, their conversations were confined mainly to being about the children, her cooking and gardening. Marta felt awkward hearing about personal and intimate information about him without her husband beside her, but he continued with solemnity in his voice.

He explained to her that, at that time, he planned to go to Davao to work at an *abaca* plantation. He had secured a job and a house, and he would bring his wife and children. Davao District had very fertile soil, favourable for growing *abaca* (Manila hemp), exported to the US and other countries for rope vessels and textiles. The high demand for rope for naval use caused a boom in the industry. The shortage of good quality labourers encouraged migrants from Japan. Their primary motive was to escape from poverty, poor miserable lives and become richer. Many migrated mainly from Okinawa to Davao who found the Philippines to be a paradise, but a small proportion also from mainland Japan settled in other parts and generally engaged in fishing and carpentry but mainly in the cultivation of *abaca.*

His hometown was in Miyazaki Prefecture at the southernmost tip of Kyushu island. He lived in a small sleepy town that mainly focused on agriculture and fishing for their livelihoods. It was prone to typhoons, although the Oyodo river runs through Miyazaki Prefecture, which ultimately drained the heavy rains from May to July into the Pacific Ocean. Still, the main livelihood still depended on its yearly harvest, which were heavily affected by its climate.

An engineer by profession, he changed his job to become a policeman after a fatal accident at work that left him depressed with guilt. He was a diligent and subservient policeman and was soon promoted then sent to Korea for a higher position. While in Korea, he was informed by the authorities that he was going to the Philippines. He was secretly sent to the Philippines to be based in Mindanao with 16,000 other Japanese, a battalion of men building the infrastructure before the war. His dream of being a rich *abaca* factory owner was shattered by this order but he had no choice but to join a group of men by the port in May 1941 to sail the Pacific Ocean to an unknown destination.

He had been asleep in his bunk when a series of repeated thudding noise drifted him in and out of his sleep, then the ship suddenly swung from side to side like a crazy pendulum. Awake, he looked out into a darkness of the abyss, then tried to open his cabin door, but he was pushed back by a giant wave.

Defenceless against the mighty force of the water, he gripped tightly until another wave came and swung the door open for him. A mere second of relief was replaced by days of unconsciousness as an almighty wave sucked his small figure and spat him out on the shore of a tiny fishing village called *Daan-Bantayan*, Cebu.

When he opened his eyes, he was surrounded by a group of men that looked like him. Unable to maintain his consciousness, he fell back into a deep sleep for nearly a week. When he woke up he found himself in a bedroom with the sound of the gentle lapping of waves on the shore and varying pitches of children's voices. This time, he knew he was safe.

Still unable to hold himself straight, he sat at the edge of the bed and with the help of the narrow wooden rail, he began to step down the slatted bamboo steps and onto a vast ground of talcum powder like white sand. The playing children immediately stopped to gather around the half-naked alien. He smiled but they went away giggling, until he came towards a handful of men gathered by the shore mending their nets.

Unable to speak the language and be understood, the locals called him *"Totoy"*. Totoy, with the help of the locals, built himself a home from the palm trees that grew abundantly on the island. Bamboo was used to make the main structure, such as the posts, walls and floor, while palm leaves were used for the roof and to cover the outside walls. Clothes were donated and meals brought to him by neighbours, including his soap, towel, toothbrush and a seashell comb.

He melted quickly into the village life and he joined a group of fishermen, including his friend Felipe, at dawn for daily fishing trips out to sea, followed by an hour or two afterwards at the market to sell their day's catch. The local life and community seemed sufficient and his presence was embraced with companionship and delight, especially at christenings, weddings and birthdays.

Yet, for him, this life in paradise had to end. Before dawn one day in late August, Totoy knocked at every door to say goodbye to the people who had adopted him as one of their own. Felipe, who found him unconscious on the beach and became his best friend, was traumatised by the sudden news. He walked away carrying only a small woven case and headed towards the bus station, which would take him to the city where he could catch a ship to Manila.

Four o'clock in the morning, his normal routine was to be up and about, so Shigehiro was already dressed and taking reluctant footsteps from house to house and on to the bus stop. Then he took a gulp of the fresh cool air as the bus drove along the coastal road. He caught a glimpse of the fishermen coming back, with some already by their market stalls with the day's catch. Wives traditionally met their husbands at the stalls on their return, followed by an early morning family picnic breakfast on the beach.

The long stretch of fine white powdery sand covered the entire length of an area as far as the eye could see. Sparsely populated, it was shared only by domestic and farm animals, along with the sea creatures that swam the seas around them.

He was regularly lulled to sleep with the mellow splashing of waves along the shore and into a deep nightly trance, interrupted only by the occasional dropping of a coconut. He learned that the humble coconut was stripped of its every part and used as a building material, as household implements such as broom and floor scrub, for decoration, cooking and medicinal use. The juice from its trunk was even extracted and then fermented and turned into an alcoholic and intoxicating drink known as *tuba*.

Totoy's head filled with pictures of faces of the happy families he had left behind. The farmers, carpenters, market traders and, of course, the fishermen's families who all lived and shared their day-to-day lives in this island paradise. A tear of sadness dropped from the corner of his eye as he left another life, slightly reluctant to take on his new life in a big city.

Visaya to Manila

Chief Engineer Ricardo Concepcion

Carrying a suitcase in his hand, he could hear the foghorn – from what seemed like a short distance away – with much relief at the end of a three-hour bus ride. He knew that the few pesos he saved from selling his catch would not be enough for two weeks. Industrious and resourceful, he planned to ask the captain for any job he could give him in exchange for his basic daily needs and food.

From the bus stop, he strode along the pier promenade to the office terminal where he got his ticket. Miraculously able to navigate, despite the absence of signs and notices and his language handicap, he still managed to find his way and ended up in a frenetic area of public assembly. A hive of early morning activity, with scattered crates and boxes, some stacked in a most chaotic fashion and waiting to be moved. There were towering baskets too, all full of goods carried on the heads of men shuffling from angle to angle to find their way around the terminal. An assortment of private companies of stevedores, for the regular ship maintenance, and shipping employees were on the move, busy checking and scribbling notes with luggage and bags appearing from mid-air from the direction of baggage handlers to awaiting ships and the bellowing pier vendors pushing their trays of food towards the passengers' faces.

He had just enough money saved to pay for a single ticket to Manila, so he waited in a back room, behind the office. Opening the door was like walking into an open drain. It was a small, unventilated room with a mixture of travellers, including their live animals, filling the crowded room. The foul smell of humid air choked his lungs, making him cough and walk back outside to get away from possible fainting. He looked at the piece of paper where it said, *S/S Visaya,* pier 7, 12:30, with the issuer's signature and the price, which was five pesos and fifty centavos.

"Twelve-thirty, it leaves at twelve-thirty," he shouted to himself as he ran towards pier 7 to *S/S Visaya*.

It was a steep climb using a narrow wooden plank to reach the ship's entrance with only a thin rope to hold on to. Inside was a lounge filled with slats of bamboo seats chained to the floor while *abaca* hammocks hung along the edge behind the seats. He moved away from the higgledy-piggledy array of furnishings to look for his bunk. Clearly marked cabins were on the upper deck for first and second-class passengers, but his was below deck with three other passengers, and just above the engine room, well away from the expensive paying passengers.

At five the next morning he left his bunk in search of a job. The captain was already at the officers' mess having his breakfast. "Excuse me," he said, greeting him with a bow. "I hope to be your help if you need a person to clean, chop, cook or serve you." He spoke slowly with a sombre expression on his face.

"What is your name?" were the captain's first words to him, then he offered him some hope. "You can go in the kitchen and tell Cook that I sent you to help – he is useless. Always drunk!"

He skipped away from the table, energised with the hope of being occupied during the long hours at sea and surviving the prospect of near starvation.

Before going to bed that night, when all the kitchen staff had retired for the night, he sneaked back into the kitchen to give the place a total debug and disinfection – a complete massacre of the unwanted creatures that had made the kitchen their home. While shadowing Cook, his eyes were drawn to the undesirable passengers that darted in and out from under the sink area and skated along the black greasy floor, occasionally facing their demise when someone's foot crushed their bodies flat on the surface. A *Chlorox* scrub, a strong bleach, was applied all over the work surfaces, then a thorough soap scrub on all chopping boards and utensils. Finally, he got down on his hands and knees to scrape away all the grease and grime deposits. That night he left the kitchen spick and span and squeaky clean. So clean that even he was confident enough that he could eat his dinner off the floor.

Ricardo Concepcion, the Chief Engineer, was in the heart of the ship's engine room. Quietly spoken, he was much liked and respected by his crew and his two apprentices, Wilfredo Fernandez and Rodolfo Aguadera. They were on their maiden voyage with Chief Engineer Concepcion from Manila to Cebu and this was their return voyage from Cebu to Manila. As duty called for his presence in the engine room, his irregular meals were often brought to his cabin, especially during his long night shift. Apart from bringing the Chief Engineer's meals to his cabin, Totoy soon befriended the chief engineer through their mutual passion of playing musical instruments. It was a relaxing diversion they shared after work. He played the bamboo flute called *shakuhachi* while Chief played the harmonica and the Philippine *bandurria.* So it followed that, whenever possible, on evenings after work Totoy brought the *pulutan,* tapas-like appetisers, and shared a beer or two while they played tunes at the chief engineer's cabin.

The weather was kind and the ship was scheduled to arrive at Manila Harbour. The night before dockside, they had a farewell drink where Ricardo gave his home address in Manila to his newly found friend. On board, pages from the Bureau of Customs paperwork were read, signed and authorised as part of the disembarkation procedures. Slowly but surely, the relieved but excited passengers of S/S Visaya gathered along the corridor towards the gang plank to exit and make their way to the shores of Manila. The tired ship's crew and officers lined up along the upper deck for the customary ceremonial mini-pageant in full uniform as they docked on port beside Manila Bay.

Their early afternoon arrival brought the best view of Manila Bay, usually obstructed during the day by the heat haze that outlined the harbour. Dusk brought an explosion of the vivid orange, yellow, red and blue that painted the endless span of clouds in the sky that reflected the stretch of water below it. As the ship dropped its anchor, in the visible distance from where he stood, he could see a brightly lit sign on the building that read… Manila Hotel.

He did not look back. Excitement and the city buzz thrilled him with the magic of a new life on foreign soil. Inside his pocket was the address of a former village friend, Tanaka, who after ten years of working at an *abaca* plantation, now owned a clothing shop in a fashionable district in Manila called *Carriedo*. The exclusive shopping area was lined with ready-made clothes, handbags, shoes and hand-made men's and women's clothing and Chinese jewellery shops.

His were eyes fixed on the road with directions to Tanaka's shop, but he was distracted by the noise, traffic and buildings – all of it was quite unfamiliar after sleepy *Daanbantayan*. He ambled leisurely to the front of the hotel, where a row of horse-drawn carriages, called *calesa*, lined the entrance, offering rides and tours to hotel guests. He climbed on one that was immediately in front of him and, with his broken English, he tried to explain where he wanted to be taken.

"Oh, Carriedo, number twenty-two Carriedo Avenue. That will be five centavos, sir."

As the *calesa* moved away, he hit his head on the wooden pole above him, losing his balance inside the unfamiliar vehicle. They left the sights of Luneta Park, the walled area called *Intramuros,* the city hall, and then they crossed the *Pasig* River to *Escolta*, which marked the beginning of the commercial and business district of Manila.

"Sir, I take you to see our Holy Church."

Not questioning his driver's improvised itinerary as it seemed like he had no choice, Totoy just sat in the back absorbing the sights, smells and sounds of the city.

"We are now in *Quiapo*, sir, downtown Manila – and that is Quiapo Church."

He looked out and saw a church that

had taken on a Spanish architectural style with women candle-sellers sat on the marble steps and others crouched on the pavement beside the street, selling garlands of white flowers.

"Those are our *Sampaguita,* sir. Our national flower, given to welcome friends and visitors into our homes but, in this case, garlands are also used as offerings to saints."

Swirls of smoke rose from barbecued pork on sticks, rows of boiled and roasted sweetcorn, peanuts and cashews, with a variety of tropical fruit, along with wooden ornaments of bamboo baskets and table cloths that were displayed on the stalls as they passed by.

"What is *balut?*" Curious of the new word from a man as he passed by shouting.

"Ah, sir, that is our local delicacy: boiled ducks' eggs."

Suddenly the pavement stalls disappeared to a parade of dress and shoes shops, restaurants and offices.

"We are now in *Carriedo*, sir. Twenty-two must be on your side because the odd numbers are over here." The carriage slowed down to a gentle canter and stopped at a sign… Tan's Apparel.

He walked inside, where there stood behind the counter his friend, Tanaka, dressed in a fine Filipino short-sleeved shirt in native *barong.* He instinctively bowed from head to waist at thirty degrees, his hands with their palms down at the side of his knees. Then he looked up, while still bent, and politely greeted his friend. The familiar exchanges of courtesy bows returned as if he was being transported back to Japan.

Then they walked along a long and narrow corridor, barely lit, and on to a room at the end. They opened the two wooden sliding doors where inside was a *tatami*-covered floor with two silk cushions lying on either side of a low lacquered black table. The centrepiece on the table was a tray of two teacups and a Japanese earthenware teapot.

It was at this point of his story that he could not tell Marta anymore and so he decided to stop. He distracted Marta by saying that the rain had stopped and asked to be excused to help Doreng to pick up the children from school.

Ang Matibay to Obrero

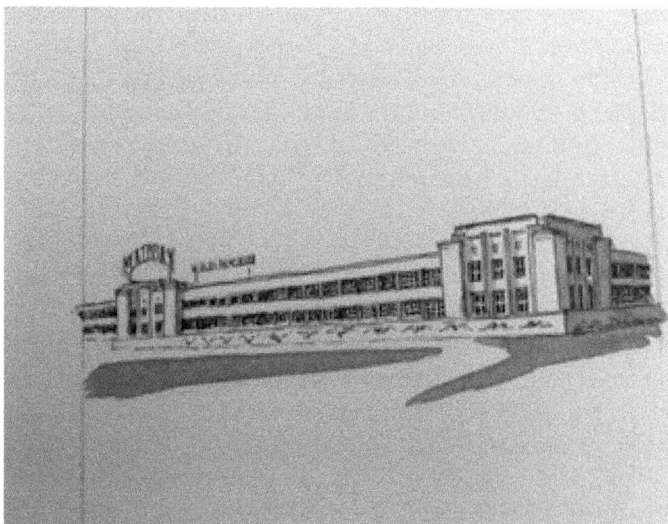

Don Pedro's shoe factory, Ang Matibay

A third person joined the two men for dinner. As soon as he changed into his Japanese clothes it was like a bell ringing to remind him of his real mission in Manila. The men bowed in front of Shigehiro, then Tanaka said, "This is Captain Uchiyama, who is our chief intelligence officer. He will brief you on your assigned territory, which is the North of Manila onwards. So, we recommend that you base yourself near *Caloocan*, a village which is reasonably close to Manila and the designated undercover meeting place for the team, the Far Eastern University. Using my contacts, I have arranged an interview for a job for you at a nearby shoe factory, *Ang*

Matibay," Tanaka continued with subtle firmness in his voice.

"*Itekademas*. Thank you for this food," was uttered by the men. These words from home were religiously embedded in their hearts then followed by the customary bow before they ate their Japanese meal. On the table, a tray for each consisted of *shiba-ebi kimpura ingen* and *shoga* (shrimp *kimpura*-style with string beans and grated ginger). It also included rice, miso soup, pickled ginger and fried *unagi*, or eel, all graced with a *waling* (a native orchid) spray on a six-inch stone pot delicately placed in the centre of the black lacquered table.

A simple homely dinner was prettily arranged on the table with delicately-chosen porcelain china that consisted of five items: three entrees, rice and a soup. In *bonzenryori* there is a definite order for serving dinner but, for the informal dinner, usually the dishes are served at the same time.

In serving the informal dinner, the rice bowl goes on the left and the soup on the right; in addition, all shallow dishes go on the right and all the deeper ones on the left, except that of the *omuko,* which is placed at the right. The chopsticks are placed at the front of the tray (nearest the guest), with the tips (the ends used for eating) on the chopstick rest. Since chopsticks are held in the right hand, their rest should naturally go on the left. In place of the Western-style finger bowl, the *oshibori* is used at Japanese dinners. However, *sake* (Japanese wine) was

64

served, so it preceded dinner proper with three relishes called *oroshi;* then dinner was served and, after the table had been cleared, the dessert. More *sake* was drunk before they finally retired for the night.

"*Arigato gozaimashita* (Thank you very much)," was followed by a bow that completed the evening for the men.

Refreshed after a good night's sleep, Shigehiro woke up to a smart dark brown suit of work clothes for his interview at the factory. Wrapped in brown paper, he undid the *abaca* string and changed into his new outfit. He stepped on the pavement, hailed a *calesa* and asked to be taken to *Ang Matibay*.

From *Carriedo*, they turned right to *Rizal* Avenue, crossed *C. M. Recto* street, passed *Blumentritt* market and *Blumentritt* Railway Station, along *Manuguit*, *Matang Tubig*, *Barrio Obrero*, *Grace Park,* then towards First, Second, Third, Fourth and Fifth Avenue, where they turned left. A high wall that enclosed the factory occupied the whole street. They entered through a gate guarded by security and, once inside, it was like a mini residential estate on its own, with rows of terraced houses, a church, a playground, a cinema, food stalls and eating areas with a long paved area in the middle that led to the main administrative building of the shoe factory.

The owner, Don Pedro Marquez del Toro, was dressed in a pale cream long-sleeved *barong* and welcomed the visitor with a handshake. He took his spectacles off and placed them on his table, pointed at a chair, suggesting his visitor should sit down, and then spoke gently. "There are no jobs available now but my secretary will give you an address in *Obrero* where my sister lives. She is looking to replace her ageing handyman and I know that she also wants a gardener. Tell her that I sent you. That is enough assurance for you."

He pulled the few coins from his pocket. With only ten centavos left, the only way was to walk back and retraced his *calesa* ride to *Ang Matibay*. The walk back towards *Barrio Obrero* was a challenge as he tried hard to avoid the unseasonal downpour. He paid special attention to missing the pools of water as he traipsed the busy street markets and *sari-sari* stores with their pavements full of clothing and food stalls. Little shops and businesses faced the main road and, directly opposite the road, he noticed a public cemetery that occupied the entire road.

As he walked closer, a group of people dressed in a mournful black and white paraded along the street on their way to the cemetery entrance. The group of mourners walked behind the horse-drawn cortège carrying the deceased in a white coffin laden with flowers and fruit. Horse-drawn carriages of close family passed by with dried flowers tied to the front of the vehicle and attached to the tails of their horses. Tuneful sound projected through a loudspeaker, while mourners on foot continued to consume ice cool *sarsaparilla* to protect themselves from the heat of the midday sun.

Local children followed as refreshments and cigars were freely shared among anyone who trailed along with them. The teenager who seemed to be in charge of handing out the drinks looked at Shigehiro as he approached the crowd and offered him a bottle of *sarsaparilla* with some tobacco. He accepted with a graceful bow and continued to walk. He was astonished by the highly embellished and pristinely presented white tombs, which gave him the impression that, in this Catholic country, attention and care by their relatives extended beyond life.

He was refreshed, but the heat of the mid-afternoon sun gradually drained away his enthusiasm for exploring the surroundings. His patience was rewarded and, with only small traces of patience left, he was relieved to see what seemed to be the finishing line of his long walk.

Concentrated in the middle of the arable land were a small number of hut-like houses with palm trees that dotted the peaceful landscape. Among these houses was a Spanish-looking building that stood out from the rest. Around it was a land of corn, rice paddy fields and sugarcane fields, with black buffaloes left to roam the village. He was instantly drawn to the big house. His steps went faster as if his diminished energy had been replenished and renewed by hope. He skipped lightly towards the gate where, as he got closer, inscribed on a rectangular piece of metal nailed to the gate was: Garcia Lopez. It was the name scribbled on a piece of paper from Don Pedro Marquez del Toro. He knocked. No one answered. So he gently moved the handle and held it tightly to slide it open. Then finally the gate's handle moved, and he opened the door to his new life.

Noche Buena

The Tea House

As clear as daylight, he recalled his
thoughts all those months ago, and he
shivered in the heat with the fear of
being discovered, his real identity
exposed. He had regular meetings in
Manila but the whole country was in a
joyful mood in anticipation of Christmas
and he was pleased for the distraction.
Four weeks before Christmas and the whole
of the village was at the height of their
excitement in their preparations for
Noche Buena, a midnight feast on the eve

of Christmas Day.

Christmas is the mother of all festivities in the Philippines. It was massively important to the *Barrio Obrero* and to the hugely religious country. Christmas Day was centred only on children, so *Noche Buena* was the family dinner on Christmas Eve which allowed parents to give their time wholly on Christmas Day to nieces and nephews, godchildren, grandchildren, neighbours' children, and for any child that dropped by regardless of any family attachment. Santa came to each house on Christmas Eve, after church and before dinner so everyone opened their presents before going to bed, leaving the next day solely for guests and relatives that came to collect their presents.

Food served during these festivities consisted mainly of whole cured leg of pork, called *jamon* (a Spanish type ham similar to *pata negra*), *queso de bola* (a type of cheese crossed between edam and Parmigiano), *relleno* (spiced stuffed chicken), *pansit* (soft noodles with chicken, pork and prawns with vegetables) and macaroni salad. Rice was not traditionally served but white sliced soft bread was specially baked for the occasion.

Desserts like *ubi* (purple yam pudding), *leche flan* or fresh fruit salad with lashings of evaporated or condensed milk, were all favoured – but the sugar content was so high that it was enough to keep you awake all night.

Parol (handmade star-shaped paper lanterns) hung at every window, made from thin strips of star-shaped bamboo framework and covered with delicate thin Japanese paper or white tissue paper, finished by a tail of delicately cut paper shapes. *Parol* was as important a symbol as the Christmas tree. For the Garcia house, Shigehiro helped Jaime with the boys as they hung a few *parol* in the middle of the patio along its entire length, declaring Christmas in their household.

Carolling (house to house carol singing), with church and neighbours expected to participate, saw the debut appearance of Shigehiro. With his newfound celebrity status among the villagers, he showed up with their nightly well-honed vocalisation and energetic carol singing. Along with the church choir and Ester, he went out religiously every night at eight, serenaded from house to house and confidently muttered and hummed even when words failed him. He joined the crowd as a bona fide choir member with his contribution on the bamboo flute.

While every other song from the radio was a carol in American or in nationalistic *Tagalog,* songs brought common joviality with tunes of old and new. Children and adults, almost every person was on the same song sheet and singing the Christmas carols. Music was everywhere, giddy natives drowned in seasonal joy as they followed the lyrics from a song:

City sidewalks, busy sidewalks

Dressed in holiday style

In the air there's a feeling of
Christmas

Children laughing

People passing

Meeting smile after smile

And on every street corner you'll hear

Silver bells, it's Christmas time in
the city…

A week before Christmas, Don Pedro
Marquez Del Toro arrived at the Garcias'
for a family lunch. This was a pre-
Christmas lunch but, for Don Pedro, it
was a day to visit the garden that his
sister was so excited to show off after
having it redesigned. As the family
approached the gate, there was a mouth-
watering mixture of aromas from the
kitchen, which extended beyond to the
nearby houses. In the middle of the
marble patio was an equally long *narra*
(wood from the native *narra* tree) table
with a white linen embroidered
tablecloth. Ester, with her sister,
Rosie – short for Rosalina – placed all
the cutlery for each place setting and
inspected the drinking glasses for dirt
and finger marks. To complement the table
setting, Ester picked flowers for the
table centrepiece, highlighted by
poinsettia, *sampaguita,* small pink
flowers of *frangipani and* fragrant stems

of *ilang ilang.*

Jaime sat relaxed and reading his Sunday paper, *The Manila Bulletin*, while Francisco and Benjamin were still out with Shigehiro feeding the horses. He declined the lunch invitation and apologised to Marta for missing the family gathering due to a prior engagement with his friend, Tanaka. He waited until Don Pedro and his family arrived so he could thank him for directing him to Marta, his sister who had given him a job and a family. Don Pedro and his family were glad to see him before he set off to Manila.

Lunch extended until late afternoon. Children got themselves lost in the new garden while the parents spent all afternoon talking about their own plans and presents for *Noche Buena.* It was the sound of the ice cream maker churning that brought them back to the patio. The hand-churned ice cream maker came out only on special occasions. A round wooden frame with a metal cylindrical barrel in the middle was used to hold the ice cream ingredients and crushed ice packed around the cylinder. The children fought to take turns in turning the handle for churning, all eager to speed up the finished *macapuno* with *ubi* topped ice cream.

As the sun was gradually replaced by the faint shadows of darkness, the visitors went home. Marta walked around her new garden to feel the fresh cool air and sat under the arbour to linger among the scents of her plants. The dimmed light brought little glowing fireflies, blood sucking mosquitoes, the raucous croaking of frogs and the choral sounds of crickets. She bent over when she noticed pieces of paper littered in front of her and followed the trail of white document-like papers all the way to the tea house.

In Manila, Shigehiro watched the golden sunset at Manila Bay for an hour before heading back to *Obrero*. He was thrilled by the buzz of families on their Sunday outing. Lovers strolled under the glow of lights and the smell of the sea, which reminded him of home. When he arrived at the Garcias', he unbolted the gate but was immediately greeted by the family's driver, Jose.

"Mrs Garcia asked me to tell you to see her now. She's expecting you in the front room."

Tired, he felt very inconvenienced but, nevertheless, he proceeded to the front room. His face went pale when he saw the pieces of paper with Japanese writing on Marta's hand.

"I hope you had a pleasant day with your friend," she said hesitantly.

"I was not aware that this afternoon the children had played and found some of your papers at the tea house." There was a long pause, as he waited for what was to follow. "They also put their fingers through some of the paper squares on the windows and doors. We managed to find all the handwritten papers and they are all inside the envelope. I'm afraid some were even used as paper planes."

He got up and left with an enormous sigh of relief. With the unsealed envelope in his hands, he ran to the tea house. The hut seemed like it was a million miles away from the edge of the garden. He entered the garden and stooped down to light a stone lamp, but his heavy legs stayed planted on a stone and refused to move. So he reached the water basin, took a deep breath and splashed water all over his face, hands and mouth.

His chest pounded like heavy drum beats, thumping hard as trickles of sweat covered the whole of his face. He pushed his spectacles up to his nose as he followed the sweet flow of hypnotic air from the *sampaguita* to regain his composure and unblock his head from a harrowing experience, allowing himself to be absorbed by the joys of the garden and the security of the tea house.

The Monday After

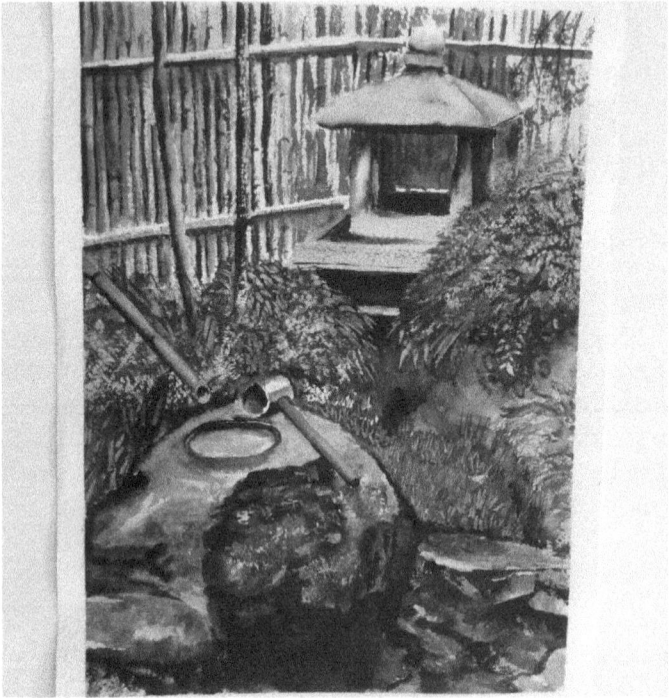

A view from Marta's bedroom window

Monday morning was hectic, particularly after the chaos left by yesterday's mischievous attempt by the children to demolish the tea house. Marta woke up just after five and, from her window overlooking the garden, she could not help but watch the gardener by the bench as he stretched his arms in circular movements in front of his small flexible body.

As the village streets came to life again, with the noisy vendors back, it was hard to imagine anything could stir their peaceful lives. The light-hearted and jovial parading of people strongly suggested the uplifting optimism of Christmas spirit. Houses were cleaned, tidied and decorated for the Great Birthday. At the Garcias', the house was busy with getting the children ready and off to school. Exhausted and late to bed the night before, the children hurried to prepare their bags for school. With extra helping hands from Shigehiro, they made it in time for breakfast at seven. The kitchen was as frantic as ever, with the children's lunches cooked and packed along with their drinks. Promptly, half an hour later, they collected their food and, in their starched uniforms and polished shoes, they left the house with *yaya*, Doreng and Shigehiro. Ester drove off in her simple small horse drawn cart, called the *dokar*, to the only women's college in Manila, her first year at the Philippine Women's College.

The Gardener gazed individually at each plant for a while in the garden when he got back, then filled the watering can from the stone earthenware jar. His usual Monday spark was clouded with deep contemplation as he watered the big plant pots, swept the gravel tidy, picked up the dead leaves and cut away dying branches. He picked each tool to sharpen then wiped them clean and stacked all the combustible garden waste and household rubbish for a late-afternoon bonfire. He felt a revolting guilt, unsure of how he would explain to Marta if she asked.

His lack of appetite in front of his

meagre breakfast was to be expected as his stomach felt like it had been sliced open with the distress. He went back up to the tea house, took the pieces of paper out of the envelope and promptly gathered and tied them all with a string, then he put them in his trunk and locked it. He noticed the damaged paper screens, so he cut out some pictures and patched the torn paper screens with pictures of flowers, birds and mountains. Lastly, he washed his tea equipment one-by-one during this morning of deliberation.

For Marta, it was a quiet day, a rest day to recover after the hustle and bustle of the previous day. She slid into bed after lunch for a much-needed *siesta* when Doreng knocked on her bedroom door. "*Manong,* Ben is downstairs," she said, informing the half-awake mistress of the house. Puzzled by the unexpected visit from the neighbour, she got dressed to face *Manong* (a respectful address to an elder male relative) Ben.

She sat opposite him and, with a slight hint of anger in his voice, he said, "Your Japanese friend was seen at the Philippine Yacht Club with smartly dressed Japanese men at a table about a month ago. Well, there's nothing wrong with that except these men seem to meet regularly at a shop in *Carriedo*." He implied, a suspicious tone in his voice.

"So what made you want to follow him?" replied Marta in defence of her friend.

"Well, we noticed that he was always in a dark suit every time he went to Manila. Why?" The visitor quizzically looked at Marta.

"He is a smartly dressed person, even in the garden!" She stamped her foot to ensure her authority on the matter.

Despite what she heard, after the visitor left, she hurried to the tea house to prove that their bad thoughts and insinuations were all false. To ask him directly would be an insult to their mutual trust towards each other, so one afternoon while the gardener was in one of his days out in Manila, feeling uneasy but curious, Marta crept inside the tea house to give an answer to her and her neighbours' questions. For a split second, she felt afraid for the safety of her family, which convinced her that her action was justifiable.

The black wooden box was left unlocked. She felt relieved as she was being given the permission to see what was inside. Her legs trembled as she pulled the lid upwards but then froze on the spot when she heard the gravel being disturbed by footsteps walking towards the hut. In a panic, she moved back away from the chest, lost her balance, stumbled and fell flat on the floor. She tried to get up but her weakened legs glued her with fear to the floor. The echoing footsteps magnified, and she looked up to face her worst nightmare and, with eyes closed, she prayed for an angel to save her.

"Marta, my dear… what on earth are you doing here on the floor?"

Jaime gently guided her towards his arms to keep her upright. Then he sat her down on the floor for a moment to recover her breath.

"Oh, I was in the garden and I went to the tea house for a cool relief from the heat. Then I saw (pointing at the wooden chest) that! I was just curious about what he kept inside…"

Jaime's eyes lit up at the sight of a large object and was immediately puzzled; how did the gardener come to acquire such a valuable piece of furniture?

Marta explained that it was a gift from Tanaka, his friend in *Carriedo*. Uncomfortable with the thought of the gardener arriving, Jaime insisted that they went back to the house quickly to get away from his private sanctuary.

After dinner, Jaime retired, as usual, to the lounge to read the newspaper while Marta tucked up the children in bed. The night was still, there was no wind and no storms, just silence as she lay in bed. She closed her eyes, felt the slight breeze gently tugging the white chiffon curtains as it swept through their bedroom window, and she felt the tranquillity wrap itself around her. Even the countless buzzings of insects sounded like a lullaby, one which quickly sent her to sleep.

Christmas 1941

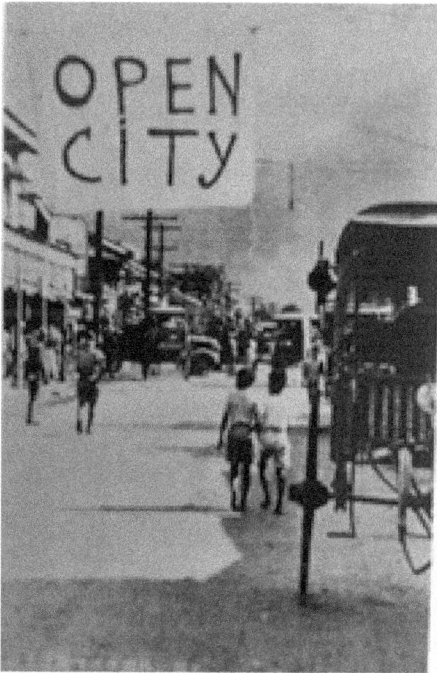

Open City. Courtesy of The Philippine
Historical Museum's Photograph Archive

On the morning of 7 December, 1941,
Japanese soldiers attacked Pearl Harbour
in Hawaii. Eight hours later, at 2.20 in
the morning, local time, on 8 December,
the first attack reached the
Philippines. Clark Field, the main US
Pacific Island military base, was woken
up by a tactical surprise bombing by two
hundred Japanese planes. Ninety-nine
kilometres north of Manila, the
shockwaves reached the nationals, which

filtered quite quickly to the heart and capital, Manila. *Barrio Obrero*, thirty minutes away, was only a stone's throw away within the periphery of the city.

A week prior to the day, Shigehiro stayed with his friend, Tanaka, in *Carriedo*, Manila. He made it known to the family that his friend was ill and that he had been asked to take care of the shop. Marta gave her sympathetic permission as the garden had been orderly maintained and the hub was everything around Christmas.

Marta had been busy checking and ticking off the multitude of jobs required with presents, ideally bought and wrapped, labelled and placed according to family member, money gifts and tokens for friends and neighbours. At home, furniture had to be polished as shining stars were on display and festive clothes had been bought new for the day to emphasise every household's attention and pride attached to the big day.

Ultimately, the spotlight was focused on the festive food, which had to be prepared for the all-day feast for the lists of possible visitors likely to arrive on Christmas Day.

Traditionally, each family from the village arrived at just after eight in the morning and the welcomed guests were served with a plate or two from the host. As the last visitor could arrive as late as ten in the evening, it was expected that the kitchen should have a full supply of food for the constant stream of attendees that came to the house throughout the day. The atmosphere was of joy, sharing, giving and love for family, friends, neighbours – no form of intimacy was needed but you merely had to have the familiarity and spirit of Christmas. The Garcia Lopez's house, an exemplary family, was open yearly to receive everyone and anyone.

The next day, 8 December 1941, *Barrio Obrero* woke up with a Japanese newsreel from the Imperial Japanese Army general to the nation on their advance to Manila and ordered all Japanese residents, except those tasked with security, out of the city. The Southern Expeditionary Army Group formed on 6 November 1941 under the command of General Count Hisaichi Terauchi, who then ordered them to attack and occupy allied territories and colonies in Southeast Asia and the South Pacific.

There was no prior announcement of events or broadcast on the radio, but the schools' bells rang and they were immediately given orders to send children home. Ester ran to rescue her sister and brothers from the orderly panic of surprise and confusion. Children wondered what it meant.

"Why! Why?" cried most of the children in the mass exodus.

At the school gate, Doreng stood with Marta clutching her umbrella like an armour of defence ready for an immediate encounter with an enemy. Without haste, the children were dragged out of the yard to the safety of their home. News and public notices followed, stating that Manila would be bombed. To protect the city, the government declared Manila an 'open city' to save it from being bombed and sent its soldiers to Bataan and Corregidor. Malacanang, the Presidential Palace, was vacated. The absence of any visible presence of soldiers allowed Japanese soldiers to enter the city. On 26 December, 1941, Manila was declared an 'open city'.

Jaime came home shortly after lunch waving the *Philippines Herald* with the headline that brought fears and tears to Marta. The headline was: "Pacific War is Now On." On 2 January, 1942, Japanese forces occupied Manila.

On 3 January, 1942, the Japanese's Military Administration ordered all Japanese to cooperate fully with their forces and threatened punishment by execution if they did not obey. A month later, a military ordinance was issued that subjects of the Empire of Japan were given privileges, civil status and rights. The arrogant attitudes and a few Japanese civilians who abused their privileges aggravated the natives.

The following days changed the everyday activities, emotions and relationships of those whose lives had been set in stone – they were instantly shattered by the war and it left them with troubled hearts, broken into fragments of gloom, misery and terror. Each day, there were scenes of people migrating from one village to another to seek safety and refuge from the bombings. Men dug trenches to serve as air raid shelters and bomb shelters while some used cellars and attics as their hideout. People moved from Manila to the provinces to be with families. Women carried basket loads on their heads, men slung heavy furniture, pigs and animals on their shoulders while little children trailed behind, hugging cloth bundles containing a few personal possessions. They walked silently and undetected but whispered in darkness about their uncertainties and their fears about their future. The city was in darkness as the lights were turned off in houses, streets, shops and business buildings.

Trucks, ambulances and cars raced through the streets at top speed, disregarding the traffic. Shop windows were bound and covered with tape and barricaded with sandbags. Looting for belongings and for food was an ugly occurrence as shortages meant basic supplies disappeared from their everyday existence. The outbreak of the war impacted across the spectrum of human lives of ordinary peace-loving people and became everyone's personal battle and struggle for survival.

On Men, Women and Children

The dangers presented to both men and women brought spine-chilling risks for both sexes. Fragile Filipino women prayed for safety as they became targets of violent rape, without any age discrimination nor exemptions, including convents. Fear led mothers to nervous breakdown as husbands, sons, and brothers fought for the nation.

Male civilians were rounded up daily in *zona* operations, where masked Filipino men identified their fellow countrymen as suspected traitors to the Japanese, with immediate death witnessed by the whole neighbourhood. Some children were driven into forced labour, taking heavy responsibilities as fathers left and their innocent minds were quickly transformed by the hard realities of life as they were confronted by death, abuse, starvation and fear.

Childbearing and having babies under distressing conditions, with lack of medicines, medical care and facilities and poor nutrition, led to very much diminished or even an absence of breast milk. Malnutrition and stress weakened the mind and body and they became prone to diseases, the worst being tuberculosis.

On Food

The bombing of Pearl Harbour pierced deeply in the hearts of the food-loving Filipinos, where food was the centre of their lives. It was an era that shifted from relative plenty to great want.

The army created a government agency to oversee distribution of food from its provincial sources to city residents. Agencies distributed the food, though they were either confiscated or the bulk of the supplies taken by Japanese soldiers with only a portion handed to the starving natives.

Manila suffered most as typhoons hit the country and greatly reduced the rice crops. They imposed food blockades at entry points to control the supply, thus causing acute shortages of basic needs, such as flour, the staple food, rice, fish and meat. Even the salt produced within the country was at a premium.

In desperation, they turned to smuggling, looting and stealing. The scarcity of food drove skyrocketing prices and, with bread winners being laid off, no income meant no money to feed the family. Hunger and disease ravaged the whole nation with many lying uncared for alongside the road, dead, left with just skin and bones, mostly along the streets and sidewalks of Manila.

Plants and leaves not usually eaten were made edible and consumed. The staple diet of rice disappeared from their plates. Some risked their lives to dive deep into the Philippine Sea to scrape a handful of the so called *sisid* rice. It was rice salvaged from sunken ships at sea along Manila Bay. Apart from its stinking characteristic from impurities, it was discoloured – but it was also rice, their precious rice, devoured with gusto in times of extreme hunger.

They boiled corn kernels, *binatog,* added and eaten as their staple replacement to rice. Coconut meat was shredded and roasted, called *castanog,* and it was used as meat substitute, but also sometimes added with rice or corn to increase volume and make it go further. *Carabao,* the Philippine ox that ploughed the fields, were stolen as meat for Japanese soldiers, and goats and chickens were sacrificed, disappearing from people's backyards. Root vegetables, such as sweet potato, yam and cassava, were encouraged in gardens if possible to supplement dietary needs. Meat was scarce and those who lived near rivers and the sea were lucky enough to eat fish and seafood. Milk for infants and very young children was from goats and *carabao* (water buffalo). In the absence of either, boiled rice - pounded and juice extracted - became a milk substitute.

On Homes

Vulnerable to varying degrees of air raids, they lost the security of their homes as houses and buildings were burned, so people evacuated to find shelter and to escape the shelling in the cities. They were fraught with difficulties and danger as they flocked to the far-off provinces or rural areas. On foot generally, they moved at night to avoid Japanese troops and hid during the day in thick forest, silently and without a whimper of a sound that could throw them into the hands of the Japanese troops. It could take three or four months to evacuate from place to place and, even after two years of cover, the advancing Japanese troops could change their lives from safety to danger. Plagued with hunger and malnutrition, leech and insect bites, and sicknesses like malaria and dysentery, hundreds died.

On Transport

Passenger trips on buses, trains and

ships were either infrequent or cancelled. Confusion caused panic. Private cars and anything on wheels were commandeered by the Japanese for personal and military use. Motor vehicles were for Japanese use only, apart from a handful of Filipino officials that bowed to the puppet government of the time. After the initial disruption after the take-over of Manila, the *trambia,* an electric train returned to service, as well as the *calesa* or *caritela*, a horse-drawn carriage to transport the masses. *Dokar*, a more sophisticated version of the calesa, owned by better off or wealthy families, also returned to the streets of Manila.

People walked long distances, for long hours, sometimes like a procession, while they carried their bundles of personal belongings. No transport meant no goods and the versatile *carabao* that ploughed the fields became the 'beast of burden'. At checkpoints, a pass and a Japanese flag in hand were compulsory to avoid delay, and delays carried heavy punishments.

There was an incident when a truckload of Filipinos were unfairly punished for failing to present themselves to soldiers, who demanded passes by shouting "*kura*! *kura*!" They were imprisoned while others were shot.

On Communications

News and radios were limited or completely cut off and the sudden rush to send letters and telegrams to relatives and loved ones caused countless worries. Banks and financial assets were frozen. Communications through radio and newspapers were severely inspected and censored for subversive or anti-Japanese material. There was no access to news outside the Philippines. Japanese soldiers censored all letters and cut off communications through the post. Worried relatives communicated with distant families in provinces through trusted messengers, good friends and neighbours, town-mates or word of mouth.

Newspapers circulation was subject to heavy censorship and propaganda against foreign news, apart from The *Manila Shimbun*, a pro-Japanese Puppet Government newspaper. They confiscated all radios but a few managed to hide them and were able to receive newscasts from Australia.

On Health

Epidemics broke out during the course of the war. Malnutrition led to a population of beri-beri sufferers – malaria, tuberculosis, measles, chicken pox, mumps, whooping cough, dysentery, diarrhea, cholera, various skin infections, boils and sores were common illnesses that afflicted the nation. Nervous breakdowns occurred among women being molested by Japanese soldiers, women who suffered without help, medically or emotionally.

Malnutrition, lack of sanitation,

drugs and antiseptics caused a major breakdown to their health. Open wounds, sores, infected mosquito bites, swollen feet that did not heal, and giving birth became a human lottery. Most hospitals closed, except the Philippine General Hospital, which was operated by Japanese soldiers with very limited supply of medicine and restricted to a skeleton staff. People turned to *arbolario* or herb doctors. Patients were treated mainly with herbal drinks from leaves, bark or roots of plants. Leaves were pounded and either taken by mouth or wrapped around the affected area. But there was no cure for malnutrition as people lay dying for the lack of food and medicine. Sidewalks were littered with beggars; they begged to hold on to their lives despite having open wounds covered in pus, flies and dirt. They ate anything, even roasted rats, to keep themselves alive.

On Schools

Schools closed. On 17 February, 1942, the Japanese administration reopened public schools and allowed *Tagalog,* the national language, to be used but banned American and British influences in schools and restricted teachings only to Japanese language and culture. They set about a program to Japanise the Filipinos. Nippongo became part of the curriculum. The national anthem changed, school activities tried to appear normal under the rule of the gun; students bowed at sentry points and library books were censored, scrutinised and burned for unfavourable works, photographs and films, and wherever necessary, distorted to present a positive picture of Japan.

On Work and Livelihood

Many women became the breadwinners of the family as many men joined the *guerrillas* to defend the country. Regular income sources went as men disappeared into hiding, being suspected as nationalists. Male lives were always in danger during daily roundups to flush traitors, and no one was sent home, which sometimes could take days, until they were forced to confess. Suspects were sent to camps to be tortured or killed. As the Japanese took over most of the establishment, in offices, schools, businesses, hospitals, transport and communications like newspaper printers and radio broadcasters, most Filipinos lost their jobs. Material possessions were regarded as unnecessary luxuries as social class was levelled; rich and poor were equal with helpless desire to survive.

Buying and selling was the only regular livelihood. There were no factories, no offices, only those that included Japanese activities and interests. Women became vendors of homemade food, fruit, vegetables, fish and other foodstuffs. Children went to work to help their families, like offering their services to the Japanese as shoe shiners and tobacco leaf sellers or homemade cigarette vendors. Others with entrepreneurial abilities made and sold things likes soap, candles and tin cans turned into pots and kettles while coconut shells were sold as cooking pots and utensils, plates and bowls. Every part of the coconut tree was utilised for household use. People became imaginative and creative with the natural resources around them and sold their products for income. They made baskets from coconut leaves, hats from banana leaves and slippers from *abaca,* the local hemp was mainly used for rope making.

Trees were stripped for wood, bark, leaves and roots to produce any kind of goods that could be sold. Whole families engaged in the cultivation of edible plants in their garden and vacant plots, which they sold at city markets. During a year of adjustment after the outbreak of the war, they learned to work with friends, neighbours and landowners or farmers to form a group called *bayanihan* where they learned to pool their resources to cultivate and produce better yield for their survival.

On Relationships

Life before the war was peaceful, simple and free. The Japanese occupation changed and took away the tranquillity and easy-going life they had. Instead, they were faced with problems, troubled emotions and uncertainty, which dictated their futures. With strong family ties and their deep-rooted trust in God, men depended on their faith to overcome the disastrous predicament. Like a terrifying nightmare, they hoped that, each waking day, their bad dream would be over.

'Hard times bring out the best and worst among people.'

The strong family ties became stronger as they faced hardships and uncertainties; they were united against one common enemy: the Japanese. As victims of the war, everyone helped as one big community of families. These bonds strengthened and hospitality amongst neighbours and friends became more open, ready to lend a hand at any time or in any situation. The Sunday mass brought morale-boosting moments as people prayed together and for each other. Life was simple as they realised that nothing really was of value, apart from their lives and God.

Neighbours and friends rescued each other in difficult times, and especially in sharing what they had with the people around them. Towns were peaceful, relationships became intimate, it heightened family values and religion was exalted by the masses.

Caution was regarded as a silent rule among citizens whose daily aim was to survive. Life could be changed into death for a bowl of rice. No one opened up to anyone, gave details or fraternised with the enemy. Anyone could be linked to being a member of the *guerrilla* groups, involved in underground activities or being pro-Japanese. No one knew who their enemies were and silence was the only option. The Japanese soldiers watched every movement while the guerrillas checked whether anyone cooperated with the enemy. Tortures turned victims black and blue from being beaten badly on every single part of the body. Usually death occurred immediately and, when prisoners were kept for questioning, if released, they would then come home thin and lifeless. The Japanese were the common enemy but the *guerrillas* and bandits also brought fear and terror to their lives. Bandits came in the night to rob and kill as no law or order could stop them.

On Religion

All forms of religious celebrations, festivals and ceremonies were significantly toned down or cancelled. Church bell ringing stopped towards the latter part of the occupation. Community and family ties strengthened through spiritual unity in their belief as they turned to God for every aspect of their lives. As human values eroded, religion became the sole comforting element that guarded them with hope of reassurance.

Filipino resourcefulness allowed pockets of simple gatherings to take place discreetly in homes and churches. The highly religious nation found ways to bring their joys and sorrows to God, their emotions shaping their deeply embedded and devout identities.

Days and weeks turned into long months as situations and restrictions were imposed on the natives where the much-awaited freedom seemed like a distant dream. Atrocities escalated as Japanese soldiers encountered difficulties and, as a consequence, they turned on the natives. For every truckload of Japanese soldiers that arrived in villages, people froze in fear. They could be left hog-tied to an electric post, left naked for days, or forced to dig graves for the mass burials of their countrymen, victims who could be family members, a neighbour or a friend. Night equalled daytime horrors as sack loads of dead bodies were taken in trucks for burial and fresh victims fought, with much shouting and cursing. Non-stop human sacrifices continued into the night with the unbearable sounds of groaning, weeping and shrieking followed by their agonising cries as their fingernails were being pulled by pliers, fingers crushed between doors, eardrums drilled, eyes gouged out of sockets or stomachs ballooned after gallons of water were poured into throats.

Emotional resilience and strong morale was contained in the modest makeup of the natives, helping them to cope with the daily treacherous encounters they faced in wartime Philippines. Like their national bamboo, they were pliable but stood firm, gracefully swaying with unwelcomed wind and surviving the biggest devastation of the worst typhoons in their lives.

Bombing became a deafening noise and the shivering rain of machine gun bullets caused the weeping cries of distressed and frightened women and children, but the agonising cries of the wounded and dying kept the survivors awake most nights. Frequent fires from bombed buildings caused clouds of angry flames and the smell of gunpowder and blood filled the innocent air of the city with a pungent, putrid and rancid smell. The streets were littered with danger, from fallen electric wires, shattered pieces of glass and polluted water in the streets from the broken pipes. The active fireworks of gunfire and bombing dominated the skyline, with the succession of raging flames turning the vivid colours of the sunset at Manila Bay into an angry sky across the entire horizon. The sight and smell of the dismembered bodies and the dying left the religious Christian nation in despair and self-reflection about their faith.

In these times of terror and fear, Shigehiro's presence was hardly missed. The Garcias worked tirelessly all day and night to hide and protect everything they owned, which they could see would be a long struggle in the future. When rumours spread that Japanese soldiers were to camp along the Chinese Cemetery area among the thick, overgrown acacia trees that enclosed the compound, the owner – with the aid of the local men including Jaime, Jose and Manong Ben – decided to chop them down. Each of them were rewarded with a tree they used as firewood for cooking.

Over the days that followed, Jaime called for regular village meetings at their house to work out several plans about a combined way of protecting their families, possessions, food and animals. Firstly, a casket was obtained from a contact and the strongest men dug a hole where it was filled with each household's precious items, such as jewellery, documents, money and heirlooms, before it was all buried at the end of Marta's orchard, at the foot of her *macapuno* coconut tree. The church would be their main assembly point and shelter, having solid walls and a concrete roof. The windows needed to be boarded up while the women brought baskets of food supplies, beddings, cloth bandages, water containers and cans of evaporated milk for children and babies.

A small stream that ran at the side of the church was a blessing from heaven during these times of adversity, not just for churchgoers but for everyone. The *Sapa* (stream) had three wells – one for washing, one for drinking and one for bathing. It was a lifeline that supplied the locals. The mouth of the well was covered with several layers of sturdy palm leaves, which kept it clean and screened it from dirt and debris. Finally, the animals were put in a giant pen built hidden amongst a line of thick bamboo plants at a field tended by *Kaka Kiko*. The men also constructed a storehouse for canned foods, sacks of rice, water, torches, cooking pots and firewood, and the essential gas burners.

Marta's belief in God's faith cemented her courage to face these trials and tribulations, and it helped her to understand that these life disasters were only meant to happen to test her trust in God. She found comfort through her family, especially in the presence of her children. Her early morning routine of prayers continued and the family worship survived, despite the vacant seat next to Ester.

In their prayers, every night, they asked for Shigehiro's protection and to bring him back safely to their home. Considered to be one of the family, towards the end of the second week, Jaime began to worry and discreetly requested trusted workmates in Manila to pass on any shred of information about him or any sightings of him in *Carriedo*, where his friend's shop was. To be seen to be fraternising with the enemy would mean that the Garcia's would be suspected as collaborators and would have to face cruel consequences for their family, and even the whole village.

For a country that started to look forward to Christmas from as early as September, it was their saddest festive period. No carolling, no *parol* hung on a single window, no multi-coloured lights, no Christmas trees, no presents, no smiling faces of children in their best clothes, no flowers at church, and no radio meant no festive songs. However, most of all, there was no food, no *Noche Buena,* nothing to remind the village of Christmas.

There were empty streets, only busied as fathers, brothers and sons were seen at doorsteps saying their sad tearful farewells to each other as their beloved family joined the troops in defending the country. Religious and peace-loving Filipinos were stunned and unprepared, reacting with panic, worry and apprehension. Although war with Japan was looming in the distance, for many residents, shortwave messages from Japan were reported – but not given much attention.

Mistrust spread amongst friends and neighbours, even within families, as suspicions grew. In *Barrio Obrero,* a group of armed men entered the Garcias, forced themselves into the house and demanded for them to hand over the gardener, with threats of deadly consequences for the family.

Jaime stood, arms stretched out wide to stop them from advancing any further and, in a calm voice, he said, "Your country is my country, your world is my world, your God is my God, and your war is my war. I don't need to tell you that my testimony as a Christian is as solid as a rock and we all grew up together in this village with biblical teachings and morals."

There was silence, and no real response, but with their heads down with shame, the men made their way out of the door. The days of complete trust and belief in goodwill to all men, especially at Christmas, seemed to have vanished from some within the nation. Despite the unrest, *Obrero* remained intact – without the presence of a Japanese citizen amongst them.

To restore order and discipline, the Japanese military authorities immediately began organising a new government in the Philippines. A puppet republic was created, headed by Jose P. Laurel. The Japanese monopolised the production and distribution of crops and commodities, such as rice, corn, salt, meat, fish, clothing, land, even matches. Violation meant punishment. The idea behind the strict rule was to make way for the gradual transfer of wealth from the Philippines to Japan. The nation being stripped of every aspect of their lives caused a multitude of problems, distress, theft and crime.

Lives were seriously affected by a lack of power and freedom. Radios were confiscated to ensure that shortwave contacts with the Americans were stopped. They were heavily guarded by the military presence throughout and the reality of a total control of transport, media and communications was the gloomy prospect offered for 1942 as it neared the end of 1941.

The monetary system changed from the Philippine peso to Japanese money, nationally known as Mickey Mouse money due to the fact it was brought with them in shiploads of war notes, which resulted in high inflation. People went out with *bayong* (native shopping bags made from woven coconut leaves), the equivalent of a suitcase full, just to go to the market. The Garcia's back garden became a depot for vast amounts of money during the Japanese occupation.

Shigehiro was among the majority of Japanese soldiers that were ordered to lead a battalion of men to patrol the area around Manila and towards the north to *Baguio*. There were two groups of Japanese soldiers present during their occupation of the Philippines. Those who were nationals in the country before the war and the others that were trained soldiers of the Imperial Japanese Army, men who had been sent from Japan. The former classed themselves as citizens and, when the war broke out, their businesses shut down, which left the Filipino employees out of a job. All Japanese residents in the Philippines had their heads shaved, left apologetically and were ordered to follow instructions that, "We have to leave, we go to war!"

Without emotional attachment to the natives, the latter had no mercy towards the locals, including children and babies, which led to endless torture, death and massacre. They went along, taking food wherever and whenever they could, disregarding any form of civility. Altogether, they were brutal and inhumane.

Unusually, the presence of an unlikely soldier whose form of arrest and interrogation of prisoners showed 'kind and mild' disposition, produced effective results. Rarely heard of, Shigehiro Yoshida was one the Kempeitai, a secret police force and the military arm of the Imperial Japanese Army, which made arrests without torture.

Shigehiro Yoshida

Shigehiro Yoshida

Shigehiro Yoshida. A military officer
with a surname that equates to being
lucky or good, and a fragrant rice field
in Japanese. He was born in Nobeoka,
Kyushu region, the Miyazaki prefecture.
Nobeoka was nature's beautiful holy
trinity of ocean, mountains and rivers.
Located in the north of the Miyazaki
Prefecture, it had a subtropical
climate, well-known for its freshwater
fish called *Akame*, 'red eye' or red
mullet, a type of fish related to the

barramundi. Rich in agriculture, forestry and fisheries, the staple rice had a harvest that was wholly dependent on its rainfall. The lack of water to cultivate the paddy fields for any extended period of time could sometimes cause adverse effects on its inhabitants.

The third boy born to a family of policemen, he moved away from the family tradition and trained as an electronic engineer and worked for a power company in Miyazaki until a tragic accident happened where a colleague died during a wiring installation for a railroad company. He was filled with guilt and sorrow for the victim's family, seeing himself as incompetent, so he resigned and decided to change his profession to being a policeman. His marriage to Kimie helped to heal the tragic memory. His family of two sons and two daughters encouraged him to provide a good family life for their future. For better job prospects, he moved his young family to Miyazaki city. He was a good policeman with an industrious work ethic, very quickly making himself eligible for job promotions. At home, he played the bamboo flute and wrote poetry in his very neat handwriting in *kanji.*

The easy treadmill of daily family life was disrupted by a job transfer to China. He was given a military post to oversee the building of bridges. He was allowed regular breaks to see his family. Two years later, he was sent to Korea as a military policeman. The threat of war looming with many possible years of separation, it was clear that the only way of keeping contact was through letters. He wrote as often as he could, sharing his whereabouts and generally any comments about his feelings. A letter came that brought the news of his eldest son's unfortunate death, providing him with compassionate leave and a chance to return to Japan. Still mourning, a year later, his younger son died, but this time he was unable to be at the side of his wife and daughters. Kyoko, his youngest daughter, was only two years old and it was the last time he saw his family.

This was the life that he had to keep away from Marta. He was sent to Japanese Korea by the Imperial Army to join the Japanese Korean Army stationed in Korea. The ship did not leave Miyazaki but left Pyongyang to Mindanao to join with 16,000 other Japanese in building the infrastructure before the war. Whether it was an unfortunate typhoon or a blessing of a storm, whatever led him to Cebu was unforeseen and to confess his real identity would be asking for his premature death.

His Philippine nickname, *Sige,* was given to him as an endearing term by the locals, which is short for Shigehiro. The literal translation for *Sige* is to agree, or "it's ok". The superiority of vowels over consonants in the local language, *Tagalog*, made it a struggle for most to pronounce his name correctly. It was mutually agreed that he was christened *Sige* on the first day of the garden project. *Sige* can also mean "go on", "go ahead" or "maybe". So, during many conversations, he got very confused in separating his name and its other uses. This created jokes that prompted great amusement from the locals.

He was among the hundreds of nationals sent to Japanese Korea as Japan did not draft ethnic Koreans in the army. Shigehiro's life in Korea was confined within his work and letter-writing to his family. At the later stages, seeing the imminent invasion, his letters were censored. A secret code between him and his wife served as caution as well as reassurance for the whole family. As the tide of World War II turned dire, he waited for letters that never arrived. While he was still in Korea, he was optimistically cautious of his move to Mindanao. He knew of the successful workers of *abaca,* who later became rich as landowners. He was grateful for at least their company, their common language and the fact they were not a Japanese colony; it would be a more welcoming environment. He wrote to Kimie about Mindanao too but never got a reply. Cebu was never imagined as his next port of call, so total communication was cut off between both of them.

Japanese pre-war preparations, through its intelligence and espionage, was vital to 7 December 1941. Japanese secret services used 'cover' to protect its activities. Japanese spies had assumed covers for diplomats, businessmen, fishermen and other mundane occupations. In the Philippines, throngs of Japanese fishermen pulled nets and took notes for the Empire. From 1845 to 1941, Japan encouraged immigration of its citizens to nations bordering the Pacific Ocean and the United States. Special equipment was sent, such as radios (long wave and shortwave), electronic devices (sonar equipment, special radar), code handbooks (Japanese army handbook, diplomatic services code), cipher machines (jade, coral, purple, red) and special code names. Intelligence was gathered by armed forces and overseas agents, who passed fairly accurate knowledge of ground, air and naval strengths, of the location of airfields and fortification, terrain and climatic conditions.

The week prior to Pearl Harbour, while in *Carriedo,* Shigehiro went out to Manila Bay every afternoon at dusk with Japanese fishermen. He was disguised as a businessman, had tea at the Manila Hotel and then slipped through the exit by the pool, going to the rocky bay and sitting there until a boat came. While the boat circled along Pasig River, towards Malabon province, he changed his disguise to a peddler of goods. He carried on undetected and the information that he gathered was crucial, telling him that it was dangerous for him to leave *Carriedo* unobserved with increased threats to his safety.

Inside his heart, he convinced his head that once he gave his life to his country, he had to be resolved about it. He had no time to think of his feelings, but only to think about one thing: his country. His duty was only for Imperial

Japan and he had to give his life for the sacred country. The meetings he had with fellow intelligence colleagues at Osaka Bazaar in Manila, people who collected data, gathered information and were purveyors of secrets, were distressing for him, especially when he had flashbacks of *Barrio Obrero.*

The day before Christmas, in the afternoon of *Noche Buena,* the day was celebrated with the high spirits of Christian tradition, except it was yet another relentless day of misery as Japanese soldiers closed in on Manila.

In a shockingly surprising reappearance, the gardener pulled up in an army truck with a convoy of uniformed Japanese soldiers and stopped in the centre of the village square of *Barrio Obrero.* In his full army uniform, he stepped out of the vehicle while the trucks formed a semi-circle, then the driver of the lead car, pulled out a wooden platform and placed it centrally for the passenger. With a megaphone, he summoned all the residents to assemble in the square. Subserviently bowing to the enemy in command of their country, men, women and children gathered to hear his public address.

The gardener stood on a raised wooden platform before the eyes of a gathered crowd in the centre of the village. He looked at Marta, his most treasured friend, then moved his eyes along a line of endearing faces in front of him. Faces of people that had become part of his life, people that had brought him back from near death, people that made him part of the community and a family that made him belong as one of their own. "This is my home, my family and my friends. I do not have the heart nor the courage to betray their love and kindness." They were words he whispered to himself with thoughts of grief, pain that made him look away.

He felt an intense ache coming from his stomach. He wanted to vomit. His legs went numb. His lips quivered with shame, lost for words, words he had rehearsed at least a thousand times. His firm hands, with their delicate fingers, held the piece of paper, held it close to his chest, longing for his mother's hand to give him courage and reassurance.

There was silence while he paused to restore his composure. He took a gulp of air, then in a complete commanding tone and without hesitation, in a stern voice, he said, "Today, I give myself and my service to the Imperial Japanese Army. I am a soldier of Japan. I am Major Shigehiro Yoshida."

No War in Obrero

Japanese Money

Like a volcano that erupted at *Barrio Obrero* that day on Christmas Eve, the lava descended and settled on the ground, with minimal damage.

After his momentous speech, he went back to the Garcia's house and reassured Jaime that their village would be kept untouched by the war. Marta burst into tears and the words "Hallelujah, praise the Lord" were all that she wanted to say. The troops left that afternoon and Shigehiro marked all the residents' doors with his own unique signature to exclude the village from being part of any danger or harm, free from other Japanese soldiers or any Japanese attack. Life continued, although they had to be cautious when, at times, women had to go in the attic or behind wardrobes to hide from Japanese soldiers that came but, true to his word, the village was relatively unscathed throughout the war.

It became known to residents in *Obrero*, Japanese money was at the locals' disposal at any time. Thousands, even millions of Japanese pesos were stacked in layers at the old swimming pool. The pool was drained and enclosed with corrugated iron at the sides and roof. A flimsy entrance was formed by a piece of wooden frame held in place with light hinges for the door, which protected it from the rain and debris, but it was never locked. Ester went outside the village to neighbouring hamlets to share their good fortune and to ensure that the very poor were never overlooked.

She went out in a *dokar* (a horse-drawn carriage) with at least twenty *bayong* (native suitcase) filled to the brim with money and distributed them from house to house nearly every afternoon at five. Every morning at three, their cook, Doreng, prepared a big pot of porridge so that neighbours, near and far, could have a hot bowl of porridge for breakfast every day.

A local school nearby, Felipe Calderon High School, was used as their head-quarters. Along with their supplies, the

Japanese soldiers left rice for the villagers and, at times, they also left chicken and *kabawan* (dried beef). Maintaining their respect and protection for the locals, they helped to build an air raid shelter for the whole neighbourhood. They used the entire land at *Kaka Kiko*'s field by digging an enormous hole and covering it with grass and dried coconut palm leaves.

During an air raid, several families used it but, as with most babies, they cried throughout the raid and frightened children clutched their precious blankets.

Ester formed a close family connection with Shigehiro during his time with the family but the aftershock caused by his true identity very quickly defined a new relationship between them. Although he still regarded her with respect, she became aloof and distanced herself from him. Shigehiro needed someone to assist him in his linguistic deficiencies when faced with the natives, especially in understanding some of the dialects and colloquial terms, so his best option was to take Ester with him around. It was not an order, but a request.

She was reluctant at first but agreed to accompany him, not to help him, but she hoped that by her mere presence, a life or two might be spared. For this, she had her long curls cut short for her own safety. One day, an unexpected meeting came about when, at one particular time, at one particular part of Manila, called *Gagalangin*, Shigehiro met a face from the past. Among those gathered in the crowd was the ship's Chief Engineer, Ricardo Concepcion, from *S/S Visaya,* the ship he boarded from Cebu to Manila. A very handsome young man out of his uniform, his eyes were immediately drawn to the woman with the Japanese officer, and was magically and instantly captivated by Ester's beauty. They were no enemies, just two friends who met at very different and uncomfortable times. Shigehiro ordered his men to wait for him while he and Ester went inside Ricardo's house for a glass of beer.

Sunday church service resumed but with a difference. Shigehiro also went to church along with his men but they left their guns and bayonets outside by the church door. They joined in hymn singing; according to them, it was 'their way of expressing their personal relationship with the Lord' and they were particularly fond of a song.

Lord, I want to be a Christian Come into my heart.

It was a verse they had learned and was known as their 'special song'. It would be impossible to think that life would be the same as before, so after the church service every Sunday, Shigehiro and his men went separately from the Garcias' to their headquarters. The tea house stood empty, the garden untidy and uncared for, and Marta lost her desire to go to the hut.

Leaves, debris and dead heads of flowers scattered and littered the Japanese garden. The stepping stones became an unrecognisable mass of black slippery path covered in a mixture of mud and dirt. Mosquitoes nested and hatched in every possible receptacle, like pots, urns and the *tsukubai* or the water butt.

The sad reminders of Christmas were all gone, but a line of unrecognisable *parol* remained hung above the lonely, redundant table, now simply covered with dried, brown and lifeless bamboo and palm leaves. Jaime occasionally said, "I hope the war ends soon. I need Shigehiro to help me to take all these *parol* down."

Doreng still hoped Shigehiro, known to her as *Sige,* would come back and remember to build a statue of her in the garden as he had promised. *Kaka Kiko,* an early riser among the village men, still waited with his pipe in the square every morning at five for a chance meeting with *Sige*. The local men learned to bow to him as an officer, a blank face without a hint of acknowledgement or a smile.

The lively bamboo flute player departed from the church choir. The family missed the warmth of his laugh, his mystical poems and his melodic and lyrical mishaps that had become the nightly highlight, amusing the children who sat next to him. The boys went quietly home from school, no piggy back rides, no hide and seek in the garden, and Sunday horse feeds disappeared from their routine. Shigehiro cared for the boys in a way that a father would. Having lost his sons while he was in Korea, to have Francisco and Ben, who looked up to him and shared their love of horses, brought him cheer and unexpected happiness. Within him, nothing ever would and never could replace his sons, but being able to love and care for the Garcia boys was a gift from heaven.

Another difference was a new church recruit who found his way into the heart of young Ester. Ricardo Concepcion became a frequent visitor at *Barrio Obrero,* to Garcia's house. His regular visits gave him secret opportunities to meet with Shigehiro – a regular meeting which rekindled memories of the paradise island of Cebu.

The Compliant Natives

A Filipino bowing at Japanese soldiers. Courtesy of The Philippine Historical Museum's Photograph Archive

The adaptable Filipinos have a long history of foreign rulers – first the Spanish and later the Americans. Their existing predicament took them and the country a step further back from independence and self-government. The compliant inhabitants bowed to another change of ruler in their lives. The Japanese governed the country by rules and threatened with punishment. They imposed rules that had to be incorporated, observed and executed religiously, without deviations or leniency. Every day, the natives had to prepare themselves in line with a number of directives from the commanding officer in each town or village.

Japanese residents in the Philippines were called to register for the military services. Those who lacked the military prerequisite, but possessed linguistic abilities, worked as interpreters for Japanese soldiers or the *Kempeitai*, the Japanese military police. The *Kempeitai*'s reputation for brutality, harsh torture and mass execution of suspected Filipino spies and sympathisers of the *guerrillas* became the main hatred of the natives, and their greatest fear.

Ester faced her days of being 'eyes and ears' for Shigehiro with unexpected traumatic episodes during their regular visits to several towns and villages or *barrios*. They usually travelled in truckloads to towns and cities, shouting, "*Banzai Banzai!*" Generally, Japanese soldiers – including officers – lacked height, but their presence in mass numbers and ferocious image blanketed their physical shortfalls. They proudly and predominantly displayed their shiny bayonets, which were permanently attached to their rifles, in uniform of brown baggy pants and long-sleeved khaki shirts with pockets, wide canvas belts,

117

soft leather boots with spikes and the unmistakable gun holster alongside a samurai sword.

Officers' uniforms were well tailored, with short sleeves and in a dark brown colour. Trouser legs were neatly tucked into their soft leather shoes, which carried their bob-nailed spikes. A gun holster, with a unique insignia, and a samurai sword sat prominently on their waist. Horse-mounted soldiers were more imposing with their sabres and pistols and wore white shirts, olive jackets, trousers, caps and shiny boots in black or brown.

As an officer, Shigehiro was impressively dressed in his tailored officer's uniform. Together with Ester, they moved from one village to another routinely, seeking to restore order and oversee the distribution of essential needs. Their visits to towns and villages meant that they came face-to-face daily with human atrocities.

Shigehiro could do nothing to protect Ester at every distressing moment. In Gapan, Nueva Ecija, north of Manila, an air raid between two Japanese planes and American troops, mistakenly bombed the cemetery instead of the town. She witnessed the bones of the dead flying up in the air and being scattered everywhere. Ester vomited instantly. He quietly whispered to her and said, "Nobody wants this war. I hope this war ends soon."

During one of their town visits, a suspect was forced to follow certain humiliating 'orders' from a *Kempeitai*.

With a shotgun pointed at both husband and wife, he ordered the couple to have sexual intercourse in front of them, thirty times. After many repeated times, the husband pleaded to the officer and said, "If you like, you do it. I give my wife to you." The *Kempeitai* turned on the husband using *jujitsu* (the suspect's arms being twisted after which the body is lifted, thrown down onto the floor or staircase) and kicked him, then kicked and slapped the wife too and hit her back with his belt.

Closer to home, in *Barrio Obrero,* suspected traitors dug vacant plots for their own graves at the Chinese Cemetery, which became a common place of mass killings and burial. *Zona* was a term and procedure used each day to parade local men in front of Japanese soldiers. A hooded 'collaborator' or local informer with paper bag over his head pointed at a suspect or suspects to be executed on the spot. At one occasion, Jose, a Garcia household's family member, stood in the line-up but mercifully escaped the bayonet.

Not far from *Obrero, Blumentritt* was a sentry point. Japanese soldiers manned and enforced the Japanese custom of bowing from the waist, with command of *"Kura-Kura",* followed by a kick and a slap on the face. The ordinary salutation was of bowing while standing upright and the body bent to about a thirty-degree angle, hands lowered, palms down to the knees, then after a short pause, lifting the head quickly. This was a compulsory practice, observed with utmost care, courtesy and respect, and expressing profound obeisance. It was demanded at a point of a gun or a bayonet and did not discriminate against men, women, children, nuns, priests and the elderly. Doreng, the Garcia nurse maid, was terrified of going to *Blumentritt* market and avoided it at all cost.

Manong Ben, who sold rice commercially to local rice distributors, was a rice merchant at *Blumentritt*. It was late afternoon when Shigehiro and Ester arrived with other Japanese soldiers at his store. One of the soldiers wanted to confiscate all his rice. Manong Ben refused and was suspected of supplying the *guerrillas*. Ester tried to intervene but was ignored and pushed to the ground. He was sent to Manila's *Bilibid* prison. Sympathetic Filipino prison staff helped him escape and put him in hiding at a house owned by Mateo Victorino, a local church pastor who lived in *Oroquieta*. A deserted area, surrounded by trees and fields, he was kept secretly in constant darkness and remained there till the end of the war.

Despite the agonising scenes often witnessed by Ester, pockets of goodwill and kindness also existed; not all Japanese soldiers were inhuman and barbaric. Ester found herself one morning in a convoy of Japanese soldiers who pulled up in front of Teodoro Velasquez on his way to church. They recognised him as their previous employer at Sun Studio Photography. To share their food, they threw a bag of cassava but some of the local boys were quicker than he was. As Shigehiro was on the truck, he got off, told the boys that the cassava were just for Mr Velasquez, he picked up the fallen cassava from the ground and handed a bag full for him to take home.

In Malabon, a Japanese soldier jumped out of the truck when they nearly hit a dog. He chased it until he ended up in the cellar under someone's house. The owner, scared and frightened of facing the enemy, said, "Dog, ok, for you." Then he handed the dog to the soldier. The soldier just patted it lightly, put it down and walked back to the truck.

Before liberation day, just outside Manila, a Japanese soldier befriended one of the men in the village and, on the eve of the Calamba massacre, he was warned and asked to get out of town with his family. According to him, "When we lose, we commit *harakari* (a ritual suicide by disembowelment with a sword, formerly practised by *samurai* as an honourable alternative to disgrace or execution), but we kill people first. We do not want to be imprisoned.

"So get out of town right now as tomorrow will be the day."

At the end of the day when the soldiers' trucks were parked in the village, local boys in *Barrio Obrero* played in the tank with the soldiers. They posed as gunners and drivers, picked up rifles and staged a pretend battle against the Americans saying, "American pong, guerrilla pong. Civilians, no – *tomodachi*, no." This meant they shot Americans, guerrillas, civilians no.

121

Afterwards, the soldiers gave them a big cup of sugar and spoon fed the boys. Sometimes, they played under the mango tree, usually at about two in the afternoon. One of them spoke flawless English, having studied at an American university. He spent a lot of time at Jaime's house, chatting with the family and taking afternoon naps with them. He was conscripted for the war and sent to the Philippines as an interpreter. He supplied them with bowlfuls of rice taken from other soldiers.

* * *

Later, as the war continued, the bond between neighbours, friends and families grew closer. There was hospitality among the citizens, ready to lend a helping hand, sharing food rations and looking to protect each other. People realised the need to unite themselves with God. They prayed for everything – food, health, work, family - and were truly dependent upon the goodwill from heaven. At the Garcias', family evening prayers continued with doors open to anyone, alone or with family to share hymn singing and prayers. People were brought together by fear and their hatred of a common enemy.

Robbery, crime and violence associated with poverty became a rare occurrence. Life became simple and uncluttered as possessions became irrelevant. Love became deeper, more spiritual and sacrificial. They were sympathetically held by the unhappy circumstances and by their faith that the country would soon be liberated.

Dark days and dark nights continued with each waking up in the morning with hope that the country's miseries would end. Sirens blared as dogfights continued to accelerate. At *Felix Huertas,* a close neighbouring street to *Barrio Obrero,* cannons shook houses and bombings could be heard from raids in Intramuros. Dangerous flying shrapnel killed innocent passers-by and *calesa* drivers, leaving horses astray and frightened. Close to the city centre in Manila, San Lazaro race track and Intramuros were targeted by the Americans due to its large concentration of Japanese soldiers.

Lydia, daughter of Teodoro Velasquez, was caught in an air raid in the street while selling *bukayo* – sweetened shredded coconut. She was thirteen at that time, and with her eight-year-old brother. The only place to hide was under the stairs, *silong,* of a nearby house to escape the danger. Natives, including children, had learned how to react to the sound of sirens. Warning of an immediate battle above them, most people went to churches for shelter, others dug holes but some just had to hide under tables and in cellars below their houses.

Adaptable, compliant, resilient, diligent, resourceful and frugal were all deep-rooted character traits among the oppressed Filipinos, but they were firmly determined to find ways to survive at all odds under the dire situations imposed by the war.

Of Execution and Liberty

War victims in Manila. Courtesy of The
Philippine Historical Museum's
Photograph Archive

Life became worse before it got better,
at homes, villages, towns and for the
whole country as the war accelerated
closer to liberation. Every day, people
died in the streets from hunger. Domestic
pets were sacrificed for food – and there
was no media, communication, electricity, transport or fuel. Sirens became
more frequent as dogfights became
intense, keeping everyone nervous and
scared. Dogfights during the day put
people's lives in serious danger and they
had to quickly move away in the direction
of safety. The Japanese soldiers became
nastier and crueller at the thought of
losing the war, so they turned on the
people.

The signs of the liberators, the Americans, however, brought overwhelming relief with cautious jubilations, but it also signalled an increase in the air raids and dogfights above the city skies. The stars and stripes on war planes that hovered above the skies and released their cargo of bombs were like silver dots of shining stars fighting for the country's liberty and glory. Shrapnel scattered and hit pedestrians, their homes and all the forms of transport. With liberation almost within their grasp, hardship for the civilians continued as food prices became scarce and highly inflated. Despite being without electricity, total blackout was imposed and, without gas or fuel for transport, it restricted people's movement. Manila was the true centre of human war casualties and buildings as *Manilenos* experienced daily burning of buildings, and witnessed dismembered bodies and the harrowing sounds from men, women and children.

Barrio Obrero suffered the same hardship as most of the neighbouring villages. In spite of it being protected from being harmed by Japanese soldiers, it was affected, like the whole of the nation was, by greatly diminished food supply affecting the most vulnerable, like children and the elderly, a problem that was heightened by an increased number of air raids.

By mid-1944, the US Army and Australian Army, under the general command of the head of allied occupation of Japan, the supreme commander of the

Allied Powers, General Douglas Macarthur, started its preparations for liberating the Philippines by securing Mindanao, the largest island in the Philippines.

On 20 October, 1944, the armies arrived in Leyte, to the Visayas island, the second largest island. On their arrival in the city of Tacloban, late morning of Sunday, 22 October, 1944, the First Cavalry force annihilated the Japanese with minimal damage to the city and the streets were soon lined with happy faces of people. The women were dressed in their native dress, the men in their Sunday best, with most on their way from a celebration mass in one of the city's several churches. Many danced in the streets greeting newcomers with *Mabuhay* (meaning, "to life" or "welcome")!

On 9 January, 1945, it reached the shore of the Lingayen Gulf, then rapidly advanced to Manila. Early on 6 February, "Manila had fallen."

"A sizeable enemy contingent had taken positions inside Intramuros, the walled city that lies on the south of the Pasig River in Manila." An enclosed perimeter of Japanese encampment, as well as Santo Tomas University, became the target for American forces. Dozens of fires and explosions continued, both visible and audible for miles. The Japanese soldiers attached big bundles of dynamite strung on the underside of bridges.

"Bridges were blown up and the city was in flames. Nervous of facing defeat, the Japanese soldiers exploded Sta. Cruz

Bridge, Jones Bridge and Escolta Bridge to stop their enemy advancing before they left Manila. The burning of Manila was a series of scattered blazes throughout the southern half of the city. Across the river, innumerable fires destroyed the Ermita section, which included major hotels, apartment houses, the Army and Navy Club and the American high commissioner's office, now the American Embassy. Manila had no surviving hotels and thousands of homeless people swarmed the streets. The aftermath was 'a city in ruins'. Filipinos lost irreplaceable cultural and historical treasures, including countless government buildings, colleges and universities, convents, monasteries and churches. Heritage art and literature was lost that dated back far into Spanish, American and Asian history.

"Success of the operation meant that Manila could at last be regarded as secure, but here was no reason for rejoicing or a victory parade." The city, with its business and financial section, was left in chaos and disrepair. Once known as 'Pearl of the Orient', it was left shattered and devastated by the war.

On Tokyo Bay, on the morning of Sunday, 2 September, 1945, the signing of peace, the formal end of World War II, took place on board the USS Missouri, the flagship of the Pacific fleet. The pronouncement came at exactly 9:19 a.m., Japanese time, where a ceremony was held for all parties concerned to witness the momentous signing of peace; a document to mark a historical landmark at the end of World War II and to inaugurate an era of peace for mankind.

On the morning of 7 September, Stars and Stripes, the nation's flag, was unfurled to fly over Tokyo, which signalled the total occupation and surrender of Japan. One of the significant stories shortly after Japan's surrender was the attempted suicide of General Hideki Tojo on 11 September. There was no doubt that the Japanese people wanted him to die. "The masses clamoured for his death." Letters urging him to kill himself came to his home in abundance. Tojo had undertaken to lead Japan to glorious victory in a war for world supremacy. He utterly failed, and according to Japanese code, death at his own hands was the only possible atonement.

Japan's entire military were among the masses involved in the war, especially the high-ranking officers who failed and caused their defeat. There were suicides, which as a race, "self-destruction is almost a national virtue."

Soon after the purging of Intramuros was the beginning of a bitter realisation of Japanese defeat. "The Japanese made no attempt to counterattack but huddled in warrens burrowed among the ruins of the walled city awaiting their extermination." Some Japanese civilians who failed to commit suicide were likely to be killed by Japanese soldiers' bayonets. Dozens of civilian evacuees committed suicide with pistols and grenades, together as a mass suicide. The

Field Service Code (*Senjinkun*) instructed that Japanese that they should kill themselves if they were captured and humiliated by the enemy.

Japanese officers committed *seppuku,* the Japanese ritual of suicide. Some officers, together with Filipinos who committed treason, were sent back to Japan. They were held in prison until the inauguration of the Philippine Republic on 4 July, 1946, then they were taken back to the Philippines, to Muntinlupa, for trial.

"They will not surrender." Those who survived the grenades 'worried' about being alive, so they found ways to kill themselves with other weapons, such as scythes, razor blades, ropes, rocks and sticks. *Kamikaze* pilots plummeted to their deaths. Although a number of Japanese soldiers retreated into the thick jungles and isolated mountains, there were numerous mass suicides within the military and even civilians, by jumping off cliffs or *shudan jiketsu,* rather than submitting to defeat. Military propaganda had warned that if they were captured, the Americans would torture, rape and murder them. They were in the common belief that they were doing this out of love and compassion. The doctrine of total obedience to the Emperor emphasised death and made light of life. The willingness to die for the Emperor on a faraway island resulted in a whole new identity.

"In the Philippines, more than 130,000 Japanese soldiers and civilians were interned in various concentration camps in the main islands," where the majority were repatriated to Japan. "The Japanese military occupation of the Philippines was possibly the most coercive and violent, and resulted in the biggest number of Japanese and native war casualties in Southeast Asia.

The first sight of the Americans in *Obrero* was of disbelief, and of welcomed and thankful relief. In the paddy fields and under the shade of the coconut trees, a group of soldiers camped in *Oroquieta.* While in their lunch break, opening their tins of peaches for dessert, a group of youngsters appeared with small containers. Hungry and eagerly looking at their food, the men without haste distributed a peach for each child. Lydia Velasquez, with her brother Albert, stood empty handed. Not able to provide a food container, one of the soldiers looked for a thick leaf, scooped and poured two whole juicy peaches into the waiting cupped hands of Lydia and

Albert. They went home and brought the glad tidings of joy to the village and beyond. That day marked the end of the Japanese occupation of the Philippines.

Probably the most surprising feature of the day was the appearance of American flags, not just two or three but hundreds of them all over Manila. Flags hidden from the Japanese now appeared in windows and porches. Homes were open to the Americans and GIs and offered anything they could find to offer to their new-found friends. All GI Joes carried an inexhaustible supply of chewing gum and

130

cigarettes.

The following days were filled with joyous welcome and adoration for the Americans soldiers. As they passed by villages, towns and cities, shouts demonstrating their relief dominated the streets with loud praises to their heroes: "Victory Joe! Victory Joe!"

'Joe' generously threw bars of chocolates and began the proper allocation of food and the restoration of basic necessities, giving immediate attention to repairing the roads, putting media and communications back, electricity and transportation back to working order. Even mobile projectors gave them movies and sound systems – the forgotten human pleasures, after being imprisoned by the war. They replaced the burned smell of the city as they mobilised their units to disinfect and spay DDT in the streets in all areas of Manila and its suburbs. Bulldozers cleared the debris and buried the dead that littered the city.

Surprisingly, there were hardly any – or maybe even no – 'encounters' in the *barrios* or villages, especially in the remote parts of the Philippines. Dressed in his tattered uniform with a Filipino farmer's straw hat and carrying a basket, Shigehiro appeared two weeks later, in the night at *Barrio Obrero,* disguised as a vendor selling *balut.* Shouting "*Balut, balut,*" when he finally reached the Garcia's house he gently moved the creaking gate handle. He remembered to put his firm grip to stop the noise but his weak hands and body just managed to squeeze through the half-opened door. Shattered, dirty, thin, tired looking and lifeless, he was hardly recognisable when Doreng walked to the gate to see who the visitor was.

As the door opened, he slumped to the floor near to complete collapse. Marta and Jaime heard the voices and immediately made their way downstairs. Shocked at the state of their friend, Jaime and Jose, the driver, carried the childlike image of a man upstairs and into the bedroom. In his familiar bed, still untouched, he found safety and security in his old home. The whole house, including the children, woke up and despite being almost unconscious in bed, they crowded to his side and cuddled him while Doreng prepared his favourite ginger and rice soup. The boys spoon fed him and then tucked him gently back into bed.

Morning came with sadness. He remembered what he felt the first morning he arrived in Obrero. The vibrancy of life, the warmth of the sun, the multi-coloured birds and butterflies, the hypnotic scent of the *Sampaguita,* the trees and flowers in different shades of the rainbow, the smell of the fields and the animals that roamed among the paddy fields. They were all too clear in his mind and yet they seemed like a million years away.

There were no vendors, no children in the streets and, when he got up to look out of the window, there was no garden and no tea house. "What a war! Who gained anything out of these years of self-sacrifice?" He turned away from the window as he whispered to Doreng, who brought him a small bowl of leftover soup for his breakfast.

Jaime's footsteps came racing to the bedroom as soon as Doreng left the room. Shigehiro greeted Jaime then promptly told him that he needed to beg for his help to escape. Jaime expected this when he arrived that night which kept him awake for most of the night. By the first sign of light, he had already plotted an escape plan for him so, at dawn, he sent out his 'messenger doves' to contact and prepare for Shigehiro's departure, which would involve a few village men, a pastor from *Oroquieta* and Ricardo Concepcion, from *Gagalangin,* Ester's boyfriend.

The Parting of Friends

Shigehiro and Marta,
The Parting of Friends

Shigehiro spent the morning, or what was
left of it, at the tea house. He broke
down in tears as he walked through the
once lovingly cared-for Japanese garden.
He sobbed uncontrollably as if his heart
was being sliced open with the pain. He
screamed like a baby needing to be held
and comforted. There was nowhere to go
but to get away from it all. The ugly
war changed a passive person into an
angry creature, the creative hands now

hard and bloodstained, the poetic and musical man turned into a cynical and bitter person. There was nothing left of him; the gardener, his old self, had gone. It was smashed and left to die by the worthless war.

To his disbelief, there it was, on the floor of the tea house; undamaged, his wooden trunk was still locked. He scrambled hurriedly to look for the key in the tool shed. Nothing was left of the shed except for bits of tools and metal objects and scissors for trimming leaves and trees. The whole structure spread on the ground in a jumble of countless pieces. Like a light that shone from heaven, he saw a familiar object, the key to his trunk.

He immediately brushed away all the soil and debris around it and quickly ran back to the hut. He knelt in front of the wooden box, closed his eyes and prayed. He stroked it like a child, pressed down half of his frail body on top and then promptly put his lips on the box to kiss it goodbye. Before leaving, he picked a stem of *sampaguita* in bloom, pressed it tightly to his chest, then tucked it neatly inside his garment. Peaceful and resolved, he walked away from his past and prepared for his planned departure that evening.

At exactly six o'clock in the evening, *Manong* Ben, *Kaka Kiko*, Jose and Jaime knocked at his bedroom door. They greeted each other but, this time, with a long night ahead of them, they could feel it in their bones. The air of danger and sadness was mixed with hope and optimism now that the dust had settled; they would all be reunited as if the war never happened.

Sad farewells were confined to the house. Francisco and Ben hugged each of his legs tightly, not allowing anyone to separate them from him. Shigehiro promised to write and return as soon as the horses were back. In the distance, Ester stood at the back, by the wall, under the staircase with her sister, Rosalina, both with a piece of cloth each to mop away the tears from their delicate cheeks. Marta was sat on a chair, with food parcels on her lap, wrapped in old linen cloths while Doreng waited for her turn with a cup of soup for *Sige* to have before leaving the house. Before he left, he turned to Marta and Jaime and, instead of the usual courtesy bow, three of them put their arms around each other, cementing their friendship and circle of trust.

Afterwards, he turned to Marta and said in his broken English, mixed with Tagalog, his last words to the family. "I have no words to say… how I am happy here… with many thank to you all. *Salamat po*. Marta, my dear trusted friend, who brought me into this house, gave me a home and a family, who shared many afternoons at the tea house and drank tea the Japanese way of drinking tea with me, the tea ceremony, I give you the key to my trunk. Please, look after what's inside.

The church bells rang again after long years of silence. At exactly six-thirty, the village alarm clock was back to remind its congregation about the church service at seven that evening. Their departure was timed while most villagers were at church and the deafening noise of the congregational singing, elated and grateful, gave thanks to God for answering their prayers. It would give them a chance to creep out of *Barrio Obrero* unnoticed. They walked across the square and along the side of the road towards the Chinese cemetery.

In the darkness among the tombstones shone a candle, a signal, where a horse waited with a set of clothes for Shigehiro to change into. He was met by Pastor Victorino, who handed him his church clothes, which was his disguise to *Gagalangin,* to stay with Ricardo Concepcion. Accompanied by *Manong* Ben, they slowly galloped their way to their destination. If anyone asked, they were to say that a very sick, an almost dying relative needed a priest at his death bed. *Manong* Ben would know the road even if he was blindfolded. With Shigehiro clutching a prayer book and a Bible, both men continued their way with assurance and courage.

It was almost midnight when the two men finally arrived undetected and without any mishaps. A bed for the night was ready for them with a meagre supper of *lugaw,* watery boiled rice, unseasoned but, nevertheless, it filled the gap in their empty stomachs.

Manong Ben left before Shigehiro was awake. It was a long way back in the heat and, to be safe, it was best to be back before he was noticeably missed by the neighbours. He aimed to return especially to tell Jaime about Shigehiro's safe arrival at Ricardo's house.

He had time to stop at *Blumentritt* to check if his rice mill was still even half intact from the last month's frequent dog fights. He stayed in the shelter of his home and family as bombings became dangerously close and heavy towards the end of the war. As he crossed the dismantled sentry point, he was reminded of the ugly sights and painful scenes of punishment and torture that his fellow countrymen and women had endured. He was glad to put all of that behind him, and seeing his Japanese friend off was the beginning of this change of circumstances, a change he looked forward to.

His shop was damaged but repairable. He picked up his pace for his journey home to tell the good news to his wife – the news that their lives would soon be back to normal.

It took nearly two months of waiting, and keeping in hiding, before a suitable ship was found for Shigehiro and Ricardo. S/S *Visaya* finally arrived with cargo and ready for commercial use. It was time well spent and put into good use. Shigehiro's papers to help him board the ship as the chief engineer's assistant were arranged, ready for him to be one of the ship's crews. He was groomed, tidied and fed to gain his strength back. His full uniform, including shoes, were all lovingly donated by Rodolfo Aguadera, his former assistant, and they were brought to his house to help him polish his act.

On a cool and sombre early December morning, the planned journey to take him away from the perils of the Philippine Guerrillas and the American Army, the two men started with a hearty breakfast of *sinangag* (fried garlic rice), smoked *bangus* (milkfish), tomato salad, washed down with *salabat* (ginger tea). Physically fit and ready, his steps were still weakened by his reluctant heart – his refusal to finally say goodbye to everything he had lived for and loved. He followed Ricardo down the road towards the railway tracks to the *Tutuban* train station. It was a short walk and on their way he noticed that two months after the end of the war, the jubilant Filipinos were already in high spirits at the sight of Christmas, with a welcomed return of a few displays of *parol* (Christmas star lanterns) on the windows. He could not erase the fond thoughts of his Christmas at *Barrio Obrero* as they traversed the railway tracks with their deep desires for different circumstances. His heart pounded in double beats when he saw the ship in the distance, overshadowed by the remains of the once magnificent Manila Hotel. Distressed by the scenes of destruction around him, he felt lifeless and angry about its reasons for this ugliness. He looked at his friend for any signs of animosity, any suggestion of rejection or hostility, but his face remained calm and undisturbed as they walked together towards the pier where the ship was docked.

He felt sheltered, secured under the

wings of his trusted friend Ricardo, as they climbed the wooden steps to the ship. He gazed at the cloudless sky with optimism, maybe even hope. He embraced his destiny, his final calling – the completion of a challenging life journey.

Nearly five years after he first set foot on land, in Cebu, feeling the soft, tingling powdery sand between his toes, he was back on the shore of his paradise island. Lined with palm trees and fishing boats that remained undisturbed by the chaos and destruction in Manila. The locals cheered at the sight of their long-lost friend as he waded barefooted towards the shore and towards the waving crowd. The war did not change them, they remained intact, remained within themselves to receive him with generous warmth and compassion. He was humbled in amongst beautiful and innocent natives whose lives were simple yet bound by happiness brought on by their naive and uncomplicated lives where the heart of family existence was centred merely on each other.

Years of running around, changing his identity, serving people and the country, chasing dreams and hopes, they all seemed meaningless. He lost his beloved Japan, his home and family, his treasured life… himself… the true person that he was.

He felt tired!

He arrived at *Daanbantayan*, Cebu, finally, to rest.

Peace is a Place

Peace is a place
Where birds fly free
Where happy children play
Where white clouds fill the sky
Where the sea laps gently on the shore.

Peace is to love and be loved
Peace is to sleep and wake up with a
  smile
Peace is when fear has gone
Peace is to give with nothing in
  return.

Peace is a place
Where there is calm
Where there is silent joy within
Where there is a forgiving heart

There is a place
Peace is where you want it to be.

Acknowledgements

I pay tribute to my mother, Lydia Galvez Coyoca, whose unique story exemplifies how human kindness overcomes the dark shadows of the war. To her fortitude, strength in character and courage during the Japanese occupation.

To my grandmother, Rita Teodoro Galvez, and her garden, where my love affair with plants began, which gave me the inspiration and setting of my story.

To my aunt, Lydia Velasquez Teodoro, for allowing me to be the recipient of her priceless anecdotes that added volume and reality to my book.

To Hiroko Roberts-Taira of the Kaetsu Educational and Cultural Centre, Cambridge, who was my guiding light and an invaluable adviser on Japanese culture. My acquaintance with Hiroko initiated my writing journey and as Hiroko's grandfather is my Japanese character, I am grateful for her remarkable friendship, generosity and cooperation.

To the Barnston Art Group, who shared my enthusiasm for the project and gave their generous time to provide all the sketches, drawings and illustrations for the book, namely:

Linda Series
Jeff Carpenter
Andrew Shoolbred
Mike Rowe
Caroline Patching
Rosemarie Brown

Jan Lewin
Mary Campion
John Farrow

GLOSSARY of Japanese Words

akame. Red mullet.

arigato gozaimasu. Thank you.

banzai. Country. Ten thousand years.

chaire. Tea container, tea caddy.

chakin. Hemp or linen cloth, tea napkin.

cha- dogu. Tea equipment.

harakiri/seppuku. Ritual suicide by disembowelment with a sword in medieval or early modern Japan.

honzen-ryori. Ritual form of serving food.

itadakemasu. "Thank you for this food."

jiu jitsu. Japanese martial art of fighting without weapons.

kakemono. Hanging scroll.

kamikaze. 'Divine wind' or 'Spirit wind', Japanese pilots who in World War II made deliberate suicide crashes into enemy targets.

kanji. Chinese writing.

kempei tai.	Military police.
koicha.	Thick tea prepared in a bowl, an exceptionally dark, opaque matcha.
kashiwa mochi.	Rice cake and bean jam wrapped in oak leaf.
kimono.	A long loose object with wide sleeves and tied at the waist with a sash, originally worn as a formal garment in Japan.
kura kura (kora kora).	An informal, a simple term in rough tone to say, "hey!" (Also, a warehouse, a boy's name).
makae tsuke.	First greeting.
matcha.	Finely ground powder of green tea leaves.
mizuya.	An anteroom where preparation for making tea takes place.
mitate.	Change in form or nature.
nijiriguchi.	Opening into the tea room.
omuku.	Relish.
oroshi.	Grated vegetables or fruit.
oshibori.	Wet towel.
sake.	Japanese wine.

samurai.	Warrior in Edo period. A military nobility.
senjinkun.	A Japanese Military Code that instructed that Japanese should kill themselves if captured and humiliated by the enemy.
seppuku.	A ritual suicide.
shakuhachi.	Japanese bamboo flute.
shiba ebi.	Fried shrimp.
sho-bu-yu.	A bath in which sweet flag leaves are floated.
shoga.	Ginger.
shudan jiketsu.	Mass suicide by jumping off cliffs.
sukiya.	Tea room.
tokonoma.	An alcove in a tea house where art or flowers are displayed.
tatami.	A type of mat used as flooring in Japanese rooms, woven from soft rush straw.

tsukubai. A washbasin provided at the entrance to purify themselves by the ritual of washing hands and rinsing the mouth of a person before entering the grounds of a Buddhist temple or a tea house.

tomodachi. Friend or friends.

usucha. Thin tea prepared from green matcha powder.

yoritsuki. An interior waiting room of the tea house.

GLOSSARY of Philippine Words

abaca.　　　　　(Manila hemp) Fibres extracted from abaca plant related to the banana family.

arbolario.　　　Herbal doctor.

bahay kubo.　　A primitive hut made from bamboo and coconut leaves.

balut.　　　　　Boiled duck's eggs.

banig.　　　　　A type of bedding woven from coconut leaves. to form large square sleeping mats as bedding and as a floor covering.

banduria.　　　A plucked chordophone similar to the mandolin.

bangus.　　　　Philippine milk-fish or sea bass.

baro.　　　　　Short word for dress.

baro't saya.　Dress and skirt.

barong.　　　　Short for Barong Tagalog, an embroidered formal shirt which is the national costume for men in the Philippines.

bayanihan.　　'Nation's spirit', is a Filipino custom which means communal work, unity, work and cooperation.

bayong.	Rustic native shopping basket made from coconut leaves.
bukayo.	Roasted and sweetened shredded coconut meat.
cadena de amor.	Antigonon leptopus, coral vine.
calesa.	Also known as caritela. A simple horse drawn calash used as a mode of transport.
camia.	A type of flowering ginger with highly scented flower stalks of white silky petals.
camisa.	A woman's embroidered blouse with sleeves.
capiz.	Ornaments, windows and doors made from oyster shell.
carabao.	Philippine ox.
castanog.	Roasted corn kernels sweetened and mixed with shredded coconut.
chlorox.	A proprietary brand of bleach.
dama de noche.	Cestrum nocturnum, an evergreen night blooming jasmine.
dapo.	Asplenium nidus, bird's nest fern.

dokar. A sophisticated type horse drawn carriage.

duhat. A large fruit tree that bears clusters of large black berries.

fiesta. Spanish word for festival, feast or party.

filipina. The term for a female native of the Philippines.

guerrilla. A group or groups of men to fight a larger or traditional military.

ilang ilang. Cananga odorata or Ylang Ylang. A tropical tree bearing clusters of drooping long stalked, greenish- yellow petals that looks like sea stars which are highly fragrant and used as essential oils.

jamon. Ham.

jungle bolo. A long, straight sharp knife used as a garden tool, a machete.

kabawan. Dried beef.

kalachuchi. Plumeria, Frangipani.

kaka. A respectful term of address to a male elderly.

kare-kare. An oxtail stew in peanut and shrimp sauce with vegetables.

kasoy. Cashew.

kesong puti. Fermented soft, white cheese.

leche flan. A dessert made up of eggs and milk with soft caramel top, resembles a creme caramel.

lechon. Whole roast pig on a spit.

lugaw. Rice soup.

mabuhay. A Filipino greeting that can mean, 'Long-live' or 'cheers'.

macapuno. A dessert made from a type of coconut. The jelly like, tender, transparent flesh is cooked in sugar and served cold.

macopa. A native tree that bears white, fleshy heart-shaped fruits.

makahiya. Mimosa pudica, a creeping plant with compound leaves that fold inwards and droop when touched.

mangga. Mango..

manileno. A person who comes from Manila.

manong. A term of endearment for a male elderly relative.

merienda. Snack.

mestiza.	A person of mixed race of either Spanish, American or European and Filipino descent.
narra.	Native wood from the narra tree.
Noche buena.	Christmas Eve, 24 December, a festival and a big feast shared by family after midnight church service.
pan de sal.	Sweet, white buns.
panuelo.	An embroidered scarf accessory worn around women's neck.
pansit.	A dish where noodles are the main ingredient, using meat, chicken or seafood with vegetables.
parol.	An ornamental star-shaped Christmas lantern traditionally hung on windows and doors during the festive season.
pastor.	A church minister.
petchay.	A vegetable similar to pak-choi.
pulutan.	Tapas type appetisers.
pusong saging.	Banana heart.
queso de bola.	Edam cheese.

rosal.	Gardenia.
relleno.	A dish of stuffed meat, chicken or fish.
salabat.	Ginger tea.
salamat po.	Thank you.
sampaguita.	Jasminum sambac, white, sweet- scented, Philippine National flower.
sapa.	A stream.
sari-sari.	A shop that sells a variety of goods.
saya.	A traditional long skirt worn at special occasions.
siesta.	Afternoon nap.
silong.	Basement.
sinangag.	Garlic fried rice.
sitaw.	String beans.
sitcharon.	Pork scratchings.
suki.	A favourite vendor.
suha.	Pomelo.
suman.	Sweet glutinous rice or cassava cakes wrapped in banana leaves.
tagalog.	The written and spoken language of the Philippines.

taho.	Sweetened soya bean curd.
talong.	Aubergine or eggplant.
tapis.	A long wrap skirt.
totoy.	A term used for a boy or a young man.
trambia.	Electric train.
ubi.	Dioscorea alata, purple yam.
waling waling.	Vanda sanderiana, a type of orchid native in the Philippines.
yaya.	A nanny or nursemaid.
zona.	A practise and procedure imposed on Filipinos during the Japanese occupation where suspected collaborators were lined up daily and identified by a masked informer, to be executed immediately in front of his fellow men.

Bibliography

1. The Japanese Gardening by Charles Cheshire Pages 16, 17, 27, 28

2. Japanese Etiquette by: The World Fellowship Committee of Young Women's Association of Tokyo, Japan Pages 31, 36, 47

3. Pacific Microphone by William J Dunn. Pages 59, p 82-86. p 91-96

4. Kwentong Bayan by: Thelma B. Kintanar Clemen C. Aquino, Patricia B. Arinto, Ma. Luisa T. Camagay (The War Comes to ThePhilippines) p. 58 (The Coming of the Japanese) p. 59. Pages 60-69, p.72-74, p.85, p.87-88, p 89-90

5. The Japanese Occupation of The Philippines by: A.V. Hartendorp Page 58, p.73-74

6. The Kempeitai in The Philippines by: Felisa Syjuco Page 69, p. 74, p.84-85, p88

7. Transforming Nikkeijin Identity and Citizenship by: Shun Ohno Pages 37-38, p.77-76

8. Thesis: Pre War Okinawa Immgration Into The Philippines Viewed Through the Life of Matsue Kanj by: Asunción Fresnosa. page 76

9. The Fateful Years by: T. Agoncillo page 59, p 68

10. Thesis: A Graduate Studies Program by: Florinda B de Fiesta Page 66

11. Wikipedia on Japanese Tea Pages 30- 33

12. Shakkei The Journal of The Japanese Garden Society. Volume 24 &, 25. Page 17, p 28-29

13. The Philippine Historical Museum's Photograph Archive. Images 10, 13, 14

14. The Kaetsu Chado Society, The Kaetsu Educational and Centre, Cambridge Page 33

15. Miyazaki Prefectural Aoshima Subtropical Botanic Garden, Miyazaki Japan. Page 26, 27, 28

16. Obi Castle Nichinan, Miyazaki, Japan. page 16, 17, 18, 25, 30, 40

17. Miyazaki Prefectural Museum of Nature and History, Miyazaki, Japan page 37, 75

18. Miyazaki- jingu Shrine, Miyazaki, Japan page 31, 32, 54

19. Miyazaki Gokoku Jinja-Ihin-kan, Miyazaki,Japan Page 4, 32, 57, 84, 101

Interviews with Hiroko Roberts-Taira, The Kaetsu Educational and Cultural Centre, Cambridge Pages 25, 28, 36, 48, 75,76,82

Lightning Source UK Ltd.
Milton Keynes UK
UKHW010711100221
378552UK00003B/487